WE WILL DESTROY YOUR PLANET

D1413355

OSPREY
PUBLISHING

DAVID A McINTEE

An Alien's Guide To
Conquering The Earth

Osprey Publishing,
PO Box 883, Oxford, OX1 9PL, UK
PO Box 3985, New York, NY 10185-3985, USA
E-mail: info@ospreypublishing.com

Osprey Publishing is part of the Osprey Group

A CIP catalogue record for this book is available from the British Library

ISBN: 978 1 78200 602 2
E-pub ISBN: 978 1 78200 603 9
PDF ISBN: 978 1 78200 604 6

Typeset in Serifa Std and Feast of Flesh
Originated by PDQ Media, Bungay, UK
Printed in China through Worldprint Ltd

13 14 15 16 17 18   10 9 8 7 6 5 4 3 2 1

Osprey Publishing is supporting the Woodland Trust, the UK's leading woodland conservation charity, by funding the dedication of trees.

www.ospreypublishing.com

CONTENTS

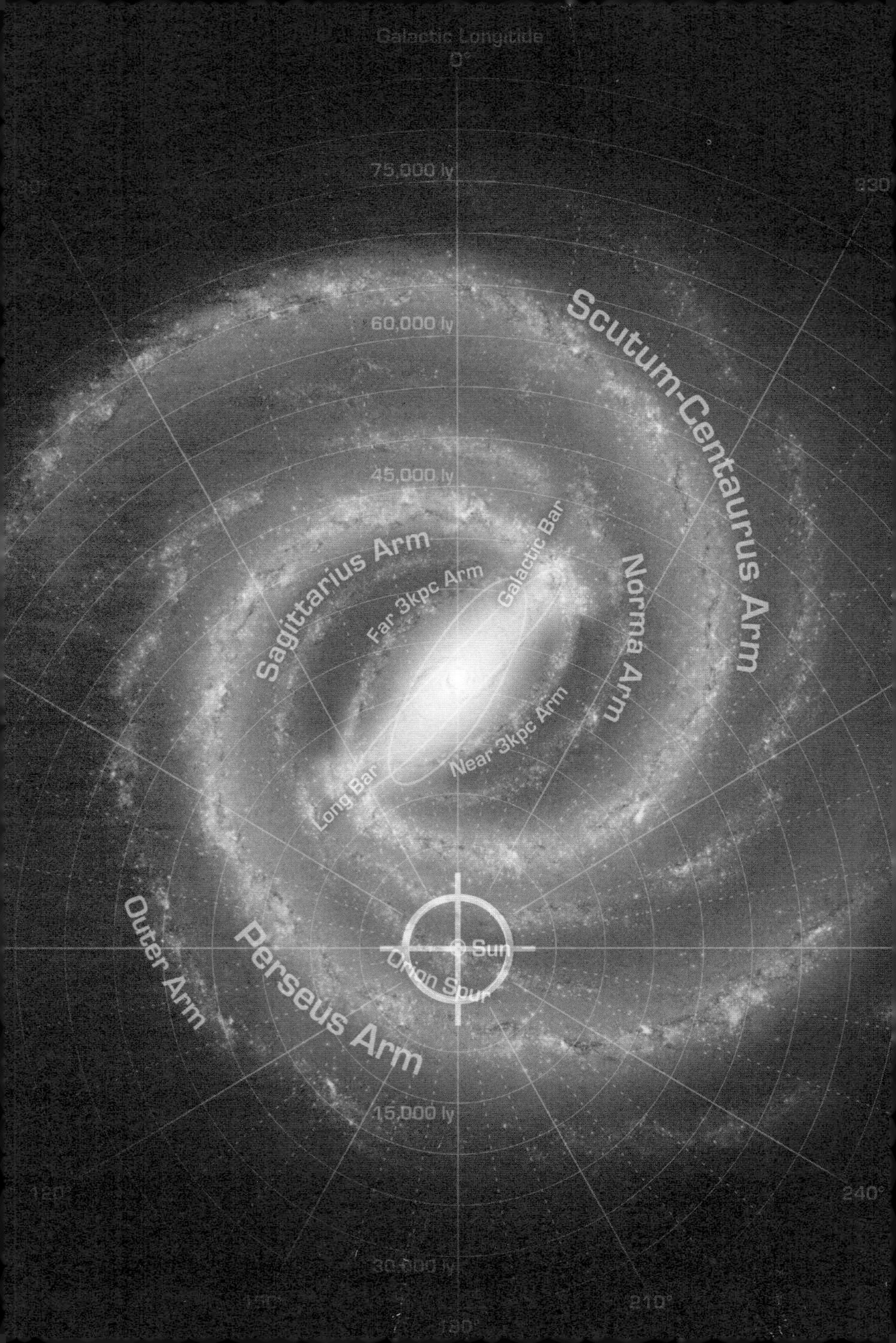

Galactic Longitude
0°
75,000 ly
60,000 ly
45,000 ly
15,000 ly
30,000 ly
120°
240°
210°
Scutum-Centaurus Arm
Sagittarius Arm
Far 3kpc Arm
Galactic Bar
Norma Arm
Near 3kpc Arm
Long Bar
Sun
Orion Spur
Outer Arm
Perseus Arm

INTRODUCTION

Thank you for choosing the planet Earth as your conquest target of choice. The local sentient population has long considered it to be a worthy destination for travellers from other planets, alternate dimensions, and future timelines.

The planet is of a medium size, replete with many thousands upon thousands of species of carbon-based life, and well stocked with liquid water, metallic deposits including iron and gold, and many other chemical and elemental resources.

Over time, records have amassed of many attempts by different species to invade, conquer, or destroy the Earth. Some have succeeded for a time, but most have failed. Partly this is due, according to the native humans, to their resistance being so strong and smart. More often it is because the invading forces have not properly thought through their plans and have taken foolish decisions based on whims. This can't be allowed to continue.

In this guide, you will learn most of the basics that you will need to know about efficiently and effectively conquering – or destroying – the Earth, dealing with its inhabitants, and making the best use of its position and resources, while at the same time denying these strategic resources to other powers within your sphere of influence in the universe.

With this knowledge, you will know your errors and how to avoid them. With this knowledge, there will be no defeats!

Other planets are, of course, available.

THE TARGET: EARTH

LOCATION

Earth is one of the planets belonging to the star known as Sol, which the planet's natives usually refer to simply as 'the Sun'. This Solar system is located about 14 light years above the equatorial symmetry plane, and orbits the centre of the Milky Way galaxy at a distance of about 27,000 light years (a journey that takes a quarter of a billion years to complete one orbit), at a speed of around 140 miles per second. The Solar system is currently in the Orion Spur against the Perseus arm.

The Solar system itself is, locally, generally considered to consist of nine planets, although the outermost, Pluto, has recently been downgraded to the status of 'dwarf planet', leaving an official total of eight. There are also thought to be around 180 moons in the system, of which 19 have sufficiently stable orbits and sufficient mass to be considered dwarf planets if they were orbiting the Sun on their own, rather than around a parent planet.

We Will Destroy Your Planet

To be sure you have the right system, you can compare distances to other star systems. The Sun is 4.24 light years from Proxima Centauri (and almost directly above it at that distance), 5.93 light years from Barnard's Star, 8.58 light years from the binary star system Sirius, and 10.92 light years from Ross 128, which is pretty much on the same equatorial plane as the Solar system.

The Earth itself is the third planet out from the Sun. The planet travels in an elliptical orbit at 67,000 miles per hour that takes it from a closest approach of 91.94 million miles to a maximum distance of 95 million miles. The mean distance is generally considered to be 93 million miles, or about eight light minutes. In other words it takes the light from the Sun eight minutes to reach the Earth. The Earth's orbit is tilted, compared to the Sun's equator, by 7.11 degrees.

The Earth should be simple enough to distinguish from the other solid (i.e. not gas giants, of which there are four) planets in the system, as it is the largest, densest, and fastest rotating of the rocky planets. It also has the highest gravity and strongest magnetic field of the solid planets.

PHYSICAL FACTS

Before arriving, it would be wise to familiarize yourself with the basic data on the planet, as well as making the requisite military intelligence and assessment surveys.

Like all rotating bodies formed under their own gravity, the Earth is not a true sphere. Rather it is an oblate spheroid with an equatorial diameter of 7,972.6 miles, a pole-to-pole diameter of 7,932 miles, and an equatorial circumference of 25,046.88 miles.

Its mass is currently around 5,877,681,383,000,000,000,000 Imperial tons, though it acquires anything up to 1,000 tons a day from meteors and the accretion of particles in space.

The Target: Earth

Normally the amount of extra mass so gathered, however, is just a few tens of tons. If the Earth was able to gather sufficient extra mass it would move slightly closer to the Sun; however, even if the planet accreted the maximum 1,000 tons a day for a million years, it would still have increased in mass by 0.00000000001%, and would only move out of its current orbit and closer to the Sun by the same 0.00000000001%. There is, therefore, no cause for concern about the accretion gained between your initial survey and your actual arrival. The planet's orbit will not have moved, unless another advanced species has caused such a move by technological means.

There is one primary natural moon, generally referred to by the Earth's inhabitants simply as the Moon, or, sometimes, Luna. Of all the natural moons in the Solar system, this moon is the largest in relation to its parent body, and is the fifth largest moon in the system overall. It is also the second densest moon in the system, after Io, a moon of the system's largest gas giant planet, Jupiter.

The Moon's diameter is 27% of the radius of the Earth, and it has 60% of the density. It has no atmosphere, but has a stable surface, which can be landed and built upon. Curiously, due to their relative sizes and positions, the Sun and Moon appear the same size when viewed from Earth. This will not last forever, though, as the Moon's orbit is in fact retreating from the Earth very gradually, at a rate of about an inch and a half per year, according to laser rangefinding using mirrors left on the Lunar surface by visiting astronauts.

The Moon's orbit around the Earth is synchronous with the Earth's rotation period, and so always presents the same hemisphere to the parent planet. The hemisphere facing away from the planet is more heavily cratered from ancient comet and asteroid impacts, but may also harbour water ice. The concealed position and potential availability of water on the far side of the Moon make it a sensible choice for a staging area or observation base, which can remain hidden from the Earth.

We Will Destroy Your Planet

Be aware, however, that the Earth's dominant life form, humanity, has the capacity to leave the homeworld and travel to the Moon, and several expeditions have done so, as have many automated probes. Remaining undetected in Lunar orbit, or on the surface, is therefore not guaranteed.

There are no other known true natural moons orbiting the Earth, although there are some smaller bodies which orbit the Sun at the same distance as the Earth, and which spend part of their orbit around the Earth. These include the asteroidal body called 3753 Cruithne, which some terrestrial natives consider to be Earth's second moon, though it does not truly orbit the Earth, but instead orbits the sun in a 1:1 orbital resonance with the Earth.

The number of artificial satellites placed in orbit by humanity varies. At the time of writing there are around three thousand, actually down from an operational peak of eight thousand in 2001. This number is obviously far below the number of pieces of debris from completed space missions that remain in orbit.

The total land surface area of the Earth is 93,087,500 square miles, which is actually just over 29% of the total surface area of the globe. The remaining 71% – all 225,707,500 square miles – is water, in the form of oceans, seas, rivers, lakes, and ice sheet. There is plenty of room for colonies or occupation forces, as the dominant life form, humanity, lives only on the land areas and, despite a population of eight billion or so, still leaves the vast majority of the land surface unoccupied, by being concentrated into urban centres which are easily visible from orbit due to their light pollution.

Continuing with physical data, however, the planetary volume is 0.677x632.2 cubic miles, and its density is 0.288lbs per cubic inch. Surface gravity, though, usually referred to by the natives as '1G', is actually 0.997G at the equator, which equates to a falling acceleration of 32 fps^2. The planetary escape velocity, for when you want to leave, is 23,500mph.

The Target: Earth

The Earth rotates at 1,040mph, resulting in a terrestrial day of 23 hours, 56 minutes and 4.1 seconds. These divisions are based upon the amount of arc of sky travelled by the Sun, subdivided. The native humans round this period up to 24 hours, with periodic adjustments. Likewise, the terrestrial year – the period taken for the Earth to complete an orbit of the Sun, is 365.25 days, usually rounded down to 365 days, with an extra day added every fourth year.

The Earth's atmosphere is 78.08% nitrogen, 20.95% oxygen, 0.93% argon, and 0.039% carbon dioxide, with an average pressure of 101.325 kilopascals – or 'one atmosphere', as the somewhat parochial natives unimaginatively term it – at the mean sea level. On average, about 1% of the total atmosphere is bound in the form of water vapour – clouds – at any given time.

IMPORTANT RESOURCES

The planetary structure is relatively rich in potentially useful elements and compounds, though not uniquely so in the Solar system.

The largest element of the planet's physical composition is iron, which makes up over 32% of its mass. Oxygen (30%), silicon (15%), and magnesium (13.9%) are the next most common elements. Because metallic elements are denser and more massive than the others, the Earth has developed as a series of layers, with the heavier elements at the centre. This means that it has essentially ended up as a crust of lighter elements sheathed around a core of iron, which also is blended with nickel and sulphur.

In fact, almost 90% of the core is iron, with just under 6% nickel, then sulphur, then traces of other elements. The crust, on the other hand, is 47% oxygen, as many of the materials making up the rocky crust are in fact oxides, in which an oxygen atom (usually one, but sometimes more) is bound to the structure of another element.

Silicon dioxide is the most common material containing oxygen atoms, and makes up some 60% of the continental structures, and 48% of the ocean floor.

As you can see from the details of the Earth's composition, there are plenty of important and useful materials both on, and within the makeup of, the planet.

Metallic elements are fairly obvious. The Earth is, obviously, especially rich in iron. It also contains a good supply of gold, an important material in space travel, even by humanity's limited standards, due to its insulation properties and non-corrodibility.

Aside from actual elements, there are many chemical compounds that have been formed by the heat and pressures of the Earth's formation and by circumstances since then. Liquid water is generally considered (by the native population at least) to be probably the most important, as all life on the planet depends upon it in some way or another.

Over 70% of the planet's surface conditions are in fact made up of liquid water, which makes it a very rich source of a very valuable commodity, especially for vessels travelling long distances.

Despite these impressive statistics, it should be made clear to you at this point that most of the bodies in the Solar system have basically the same chemical and elemental composition, but do not have a sentient native species, or, indeed, any known life forms. Likewise, the various comets and asteroids in the system are also very rich in iron and other metallic elements, and these would be far easier to acquire, mine and process, than an entire populated planet.

Water is also available in reasonable quantities on the Moon, Mars, Europa, and in comets. It is true that the amount of water in these other locations is far less than on Earth, but the amount of it on Earth is so great that removing it would be somewhat problematic, due to its bulk and mass. You could fill thousands of mile-wide ships and still not have made a noticeable difference to the Earth's sea level. Always assuming, that is, that you can get such a large ship with such a large mass on the surface in the first place.

LIFE FORMS

The Earth is teeming with life in many forms, however all, as far as is known, are made from organic structures based around the element carbon. There are many different types of life form, from single-celled organisms, through microscopic virii, plants, lichens, fungi, insects, fish, reptiles, mammals, birds... As of 2011, it was estimated that there are around 9 million species on Earth.

We Will Destroy Your Planet

The greatest number of animal – i.e. ambulatory and able to move around under their own power – species is in the insect kingdom. Most of them are so small you won't notice them, but there are over a million different species of insects. Mammals, although the dominant species on the planet in terms of size and intelligence, are the smallest group, with just over 5,000 species.

The number of true sentient species on the planet is somewhat open to debate, partly because of differences of opinion over what constitutes sentience, and partly because the dominant life form – humanity, a bipedal upright type of largely hairless ape – is extremely parochial and has a very self-centred view of their world. It is becoming increasingly acknowledged among educated humans, however, that there are other sentient species sharing the planet with them.

As well as other species of ape, some of which have been taught sophisticated forms of communication, it is considered that some cetacean (ocean-based mammals) species, and dolphins in particular, are at least as intelligent as humans.

GETTING THERE

FROM ANOTHER PLANET

Space is as big as they say, and it's very important to decide upon the means of traversing such huge distances that will best suit your species and your battle plans.

If you hope to establish a system of being able to provide regular supplies and reinforcements, and to transport prisoners or resources back to your home, you will definitely need some form of faster-than-light travel, be it by warping space or using wormholes, so that there is effectively a shorter distance between your home and Earth, or by hyperspatial drive that allows you to slip outside the usual rules of the universe and move more quickly than light could under the physical laws of normal space.

Even Earth's scientists have established the existence of tiny wormholes, connecting the Earth to the Sun, in one case, but none large enough to travel through. However, if you have developed a technology that allows for the transmission of matter across space – or, better still, that breaks down matter into a data stream that can be reassembled somehow at the destination – you may find it worth trying to combine that technology with wormholes, in order to transmit your forces directly from your planet to Earth, without having to worry about building or navigating ships in between.

If you have not yet achieved a level of technology that allows for such molecular reintegration, it would also be worth looking into transmitting data in the guise of signals to be decrypted, which would include the schematics for autonomous AIs and the programming to operate them. Humanity could then construct such machines, which would follow your programming. This is also a good way to prepare the planet for your arrival after a longer relativistic journey, if you do not have faster-than-light travel.

Such slower forms of approach by starship would require – unless you are a race of very long-lived individuals – either some form of suspended animation for your forces, so that they don't age and die during the years, potentially even centuries or millennia, that it would take to get there, or a generational starship, in which the occupants breed under controlled conditions, and each new generation is trained for its part in the mission.

These are perhaps the most easily practicable types of travel to Earth, especially for those of relatively limited technological development, but they have the disadvantage of requiring you to bring along everything you could possibly ever need – which means a very large ship or fleet in the first place. This approach is perhaps best used by those who have lost their homeworld and are looking for a new one, or by those who are nomadic, and so, again, have no home to require backup from.

It is also possible that you are a naturally spaceborne species, which requires no separate artificial means of space travel. In this instance, it would seem unlikely that you would actually need to visit a planetary surface at all – and, indeed, may not be physically able to – but if you do have an ability or requirement to visit the Earth, then it's best to proceed at your own natural pace.

Whatever your specific type of space travel, if you're coming by starship or natural spaceborne ability, your initial approach to the Earth before landing would best be made from inside the Earth's orbit, which means cutting across the planet's orbital from the far side of the Sun. You should then approach the planet from the southern side of the planet's equator, with the Sun behind you. Your target area should be a region on the surface just on the sunward side of the day/night terminator, where the Sun is just rising.

If you have already, through reconnaissance, chosen a particular landing area, you will have to time the approach correctly to descend just after sunrise. If you have agents or sensors on the surface ahead of your force's arrival, you should have them direct you to approach on west-south-west course as seen from the surface.

This will minimize your chances of being detected on approach, even by infrared telescopes and other of the Earth's most sophisticated scanning equipment. A recent asteroid explosion in the Earth's atmosphere took the inhabitants completely by surprise by approaching from this very angle.

Depending on how many ships you have brought, and their size and mass, it may be necessary to station some of them offworld, either as a relay point, command and control centre, observation post, or simply because they are too large to land safely. The best locations in which to station such vessels out of the line of fire from Earth are either on the dark side of the Moon – which has the advantage of allowing a surface landing – or at one of the Lagrange points in either the Solar-Earth or Earth-Moon orbital relationships.

The Lagrange points are five points around the orbits of a related pair of astronomical bodies, one of which orbits the other. In these five locations, a small body can maintain a stable position relative to both. In the case of the Earth, there are two relevant relationships to consider: The Earth's orbit around the Sun, and the Moon's orbit around the Earth. Each of these orbital relationships has its own set of Lagrange points.

Three of the points require effort to maintain that stable position. The L1 point is close to the orbiting body (the Earth in the Sun-Earth relationship, and the Moon in the Earth-Moon one), where its gravitational field balances out the gravitational pull of the larger body. Here the orbiting body's gravity increases the orbital period of a smaller body – such as a ship – to the point where said ship will have the same orbital period as that body. Where the Sun-Earth relationship is concerned, this point is about one million miles sunwards of the Earth.

The L2 point is directly opposite L1 but on the other side of the orbiting body – or a million miles outward from the Earth. L3 is in the same position as the orbiting body, but directly opposite on the far side of the parent body – i.e. 93 million miles from the opposite side of the Sun.

Of these three Sun-Earth points, L3 is particularly unstable, partly because the Earth's orbit is elliptical rather than circular, and partly because the gravitational effects of the other planets, especially Venus, affect it. Before these facts were confirmed, human storytellers liked to imagine there could be some kind of alternate Earth at the Sun-Earth L3 position, however this is neither the case nor even possible. The L1, 2 and 3 points in the Earth-Moon system are unstable and move around, as the Moon is also in an elliptical orbit. Your navigators should be able to work out the relevant positions.

Anything parked in the Earth-Moon L1 or L3 points would be highly detectable from Earth, and neither are strategically wise choices, for that reason. There is also usually a space observatory maintained by humanity at the Lunar L1 position, whose absence or damage would be noticed, as would a neighbour. The Lunar L2 position is a better option, as it is on the far side of the Moon, but simply landing on the dark side of the Moon would be more energy efficient.

The best positions, however, in which to park your ships are the two so-called Trojan points, at L4 and L5: 60 degrees of arc ahead of and behind the Earth's orbit, and the same position in the Moon's orbit around the Earth. Small bodies can maintain stable position at either of these positions, and the positions are far more fixed and stable than any of the other three.

Obviously, positioning ships at the Earth-Moon L4 and L5 positions, with a base on the Moon itself, gives a good range of coverage relatively close to the Earth, with low energy requirements for station-keeping. These positions may, however, be within missile range of Earth's defences. The Sun-Earth L4 and L5 positions would certainly be safer, but have the disadvantage of being much further away.

Ultimately, the choice is yours.

FROM A PARALLEL DIMENSION

If you are coming from a parallel universe or dimension, it is unlikely that you will need to consider planetary defences, as you will be able to materialize on the surface, in the ocean, or

The Target: Earth

within the atmosphere. Depending on your type of species, you will need to establish by testing with scouts or reconnaissance drones exactly where and in what environment you will arrive. You may have to cross from a specific area or set of circumstances in your home dimension, or you may not.

If your species is not human, but either a different terrestrial species that gained dominant sentience ahead of humans, or some form of supernatural entity, you will have to be extra careful about being detected upon arrival, lest you alert human security forces, or, indeed, find yourself a subject for study and experimentation.

In particular, if your species relies on innate abilities that humans could take for supernatural powers, you may not need traditional technology to move between dimensions, though it is always possible that establishing some form of mental link with humans on the target side of a dimensional bridge may help form a bridgehead. If nothing else, playing the part of a deity or similar entity will help smooth the process of intelligence gathering about your target area.

It is possible for time travel to result in the creation of parallel worlds, or at least the branching off of parallel timelines. If this is the case between your home dimension and the current Earth, you may be able to effect a transition from one timeline to the other by travelling in time and undoing the event that created the parallel timeline.

This is a dangerous route to take, however, due to the risk of paradox, potentially resulting in either you never having existed, or creating a closed loop in which your actions are what created the timeline you originated from. This has especially been seen to happen when time travellers from the future attempt to change a past or present effect, where the unpleasant timeline is the result of violence in the target time zone.

FROM THE PAST

This is possibly the simplest journey, unless you actually want to make a return trip after acquiring modern or future resources. Simply wait. Or, if you won't live long enough, build a suspended animation facility and ensure that you and your armed forces are preserved in a safe location – ideally in sealed caves, an underwater city, or an orbiting or Lunar facility – to be awakened at the appropriate time.

You can either set some kind of timing mechanism to awaken you after a set geological age, or program your computers to awaken you when a specific set of circumstances has been achieved. Please be aware that if you are from the far distant past of the Earth, the climate will certainly have changed, and possibly the actual biosphere as a whole. In particular, the levels of oxygen are presently very different today than in the past, with the percentage of oxygen in the atmosphere having peaked 300 million years ago at 36%, almost double its present concentration.

Therefore, just because you are also native to the Earth at a point in its history, this does not mean that you will not necessarily need life-support apparatus, or a plan to re-engineer the atmosphere.

Alternatively, and if you are not an Earth native species, you could skip ahead through time on your journey by skimming close enough to the event horizon of a black hole. As all spacefaring races know, black holes are created when supermassive stars, hundreds of times the size and mass of Earth's parent star, collapse under their own gravity. Such a star collapses so far, in fact, that it is compressed into a singularity, a mathematical point with infinite mass and no physical dimensions to speak of. This mass also curves space-time infinitely, basically punching a hole in the fabric of space-time itself, with a deep gravity well surrounding it.

The Target: Earth

Gravity wells curve time as well as space. Basically, gravity makes time slow down. If the crew of a ship outside a black hole's gravity well could see into a ship that was falling into the hole, they would see everything in that other ship slowing down. By the time it passed over the event horizon, and reached the singularity, time would have stopped for the crew of that ship.

To the crew of the falling ship, everything would have seemed normal, with the outside universe suddenly speeding up and winking out. Assuming, that is, that they weren't killed by the extreme radiation, and the tidal forces even at the subatomic level.

If you hope to return to your native time in the past afterwards, then simply consult the following section on travelling from the future. Do bear in mind, though, that if you succeed in travelling both ways, you may well find that the future you travelled into now won't actually happen.

FROM THE FUTURE

If you are attempting to invade the Earth from the future, whether it be from a future Earth or some other planet, you will find that your best chance of moving to the 21st century (or any other point in Earth's history) will be by utilizing the effects of dense mass to bend space. Since space-time is curved, bending space also bends time.

In order to bend space-time far enough to carry vessels safely through time into the past (the future is less of a problem, as everything is already travelling that way), you will require astronomically massive objects to exploit. Black holes and singularities are often considered popular choices, especially if they are rotating, but you really would be better off with a Kerr Ring – this would be a super-dense ring made from a neutron star – the size of an asteroid, but with the mass of a star. It is possible that a sufficiently fast-rotating object of this nature would be unable to form a true singularity, but instead become a ring, due to centrifugal force counteracting just enough of the gravity. In theory, this could then be flown through, and some believe that you could come out in the past or future. As yet no Kerr Rings are known, but please feel free to supply appropriate navigational charts if you find one on your journey.

The same effect is more likely to occur with a rotating black hole. Since pretty much all astronomical bodies rotate, it is reasonable to expect that the objects they might collapse into will continue to do so.

Another option is the creation of a Tipler Cylinder, or sometimes called a Kerr-Tipler mechanism. For this you will need a cylinder of infinite length, made of something very dense and massive, such as material from a neutron star, whose gravity well would curve space-time along its axis, essentially making a road back through time. Since an infinite length is impractical for construction, it has been suggested that when the cylinder is spun around its longitudinal axis fast enough, it should generate a closed timelike curve within the cylinder's gravity well, enabling a vessel to travel back in time along the curve.

Wormholes are also a potential means of time travel, since if they connect two regions of space-time together, then that may well be two times as well as, or instead of, two spatial regions. In essence this would form a time tunnel, or a time corridor, and in fact is the closest approximation to what some with a vested interest in time travel call the time vortex.

It's entirely likely, however, that you have your own technological means of travelling through time; the important thing is the destination, and to that end, this guide is geared towards Earth in the early 21st century, by the standard calendar (one of many) used on the planet.

The most important thing to remember is to make sure not to encounter your own selves, especially if you are only travelling within your own lifetime, or have made the time journey more than once. This can be a big problem, not just for the creation of paradoxes, and potentially alternate timelines, but also because of the danger of shorting out the kinetic energy stored in temporal distances between yourselves.

Or, to put it the Australian way, zap.

DEFENCES

DEFENCES OF THE EARTH AGAINST SPACEBORNE ASSAULT

None. Zero. Zip. Nada.

Yes, you read that right. Amazingly, the planet has no energy shielding, no starships, no minefield, and no detection or early warning grid for vessels entering the system. What little – and it is *very* little – planetary early warning and defence planning programmes the Earth has are geared solely to the problem of near-Earth asteroids, which could easily prove a danger to cities, nations, and ultimately native life itself.

This is another reason why the Earth makes such a tempting target; Although the dominant species is known to be aggressive and stubborn, they have no defences against incursion either from other spatial locations, alternate dimensions, or different eras. The doctrinal requirement for surprise is therefore a relatively easy one to fulfil.

It is true that humanity has missiles capable of being fired at targets in space, and these missiles are the limit of Earth's technology in this regard. While it is certainly true that Earth's forces have quite perfected the reliability of missiles for use against land, sea, and atmospheric vehicles, and have expanded into the matter of orbital rockets and even anti-satellite weapons, their missiles are all powered by chemical motors of one kind or another.

Whether liquid fuelled or solid fuelled, rockets all depend upon burning chemical compounds to institute a Newtonian reaction, forcing exhaust out the back in order to propel the missile forward. Although ion engines have been built on Earth, they are used only for manoeuvring of satellites, and not for main propulsion, because they simply are not fast enough. Even the rockets, however, do not have sufficient speed and manoeuvrability to be a significant threat to navigable spacecraft. Any rockets or missiles thus launched at your ships or landing craft will be seen coming, if you're paying attention, and easily destroyed or avoided.

Experiments with energy weapons, such as X-ray lasers, are currently at a very early stage of development, and very much confined to static installations. They are not manoeuvrable, and are of no threat to your forces.

All that said, the Earth does in fact have one effective, if entirely accidental and coincidental, defensive barrier that your starship navigators must be aware of: space junk.

The planet is surrounded, in bands at various heights and orbits, by clouds of debris left by previous space missions and satellite collisions, which have formed into belts of dangerous metal, plastic, and ceramics. The Earth's spaceflight authorities admit that there may be tens of millions of pieces of debris in orbit, ranging from dead satellites and rocket fuel tanks weighing several tons, down to fragments of solar panels and foil insulation, and even paint flecks, just millimetres across.

Even human space travellers have discovered that all these fragments, regardless of size, are dangerous. A couple of decades ago, human space vessels could simply move out of the way of approaching debris, but now there is so much of it, in some orbits, that this is not always possible, and the occupants of manned ships and stations sometimes have to literally take shelter and just hope and pray that nothing that is about to hit them kills them.

A fleck of paint smaller than the size of the word 'paint' on this page, travelling at 24,750 miles per hour, has been known to take out a vessel's window panel that was designed to withstand the heat and stresses of re-entry through the atmosphere from orbit. These bands of debris are potentially dangerous, and must be taken into account if you are going to attempt any form of landing from space.

Invading and subduing or destroying Earth and its people will not be a matter of fighting your way to the homeworld of the civilization, and then trying to establish a foothold there. There is no resistance to any approach to the planet, and so any operation to capture or destroy it will only be a matter of consolidating a successful arrival.

That said, there are some military groups and organizations who will certainly be the first ones to take an interest in your arrival. There are few, if any, terrestrial military or intelligence organizations devoted to protecting the Earth from assault from offworld, although rumours and stories of such secret units have persisted for several decades at least. However, there are some militaries and governments whose mandate does – or at least may – specifically cover eventualities such as alien invasion.

THE UNITED STATES AIR FORCE

The United States Air Force (USAF) is the most advanced military aviation service on the planet, though not the largest, which is the Chinese Air Force. The USAF is tied very closely with America's National Aeronautics and Space Administration (NASA) which has mounted the most successful space missions from the Earth to other planets in the Solar system. For many years, most of NASA's space travellers and test pilots were assigned from the USAF, though this policy has been relaxed, with people from other services and even civilians allowed to participate in offworld missions.

The USAF was instrumental in developing air-launched anti-satellite weapons, which could be adapted to attack descending ships on attack missions, or even spacecraft in close orbit of the planet. Along with the US Navy, they have tested laser weapons, though these have so far been clumsy and not suited to tracking manoeuvrable vessels.

Some decades ago, the USAF conducted Project Blue Book, a study into UFO sightings and reports of alien incursions.

The USAF is also the parent organization of the US Space Command. As the name implies, this group deals with both military applications in space, and threats from space. Ordinarily this means natural bodies such as asteroids and meteors, and ballistic projectiles launched into orbit from other terrestrial nations. Nevertheless, this means they are the military service most likely to detect and attempt to intervene with your approach.

This is especially the case if you attempt to visit Earth by means of a pre-existing network of wormholes.

THE BRITISH ARMY

Although Britain is a small island whose empire has fallen, and whose power has waned, the British Army has extensive experience in successful defences against invasion by the rest of the planet, and in conducting its own successful colonizations.

Since the 1950s, the Army has been shown to have been involved in dealing with several possible extraterrestrial incursions, from defending the historic Westminster Cathedral to the notorious Hobbs Lane incident.

THE UNITED NATIONS

Although it is not strictly a military organization, the UN does sometimes provide an umbrella banner for military peacekeeping operations in various nations. These forces are drawn from different national militaries across the globe. It is therefore quite possible that, in response to your campaign of conquest, the UN could arrange for the alliances of multiple national militaries against you.

Between 1968 and the early 2000s there were several TV reports broadcast on Earth, and books written on the subject, which suggested that the UN did have intelligence-gathering taskforce and response units, based across several of the world's regions, which was in fact instrumental in both investigating and dealing with both extraterrestrial and other scientific threats over many years.

In the past decade or so, however, the UN has denied the veracity of any and all such stories and vehemently objected to being referred to as a facilitator for such a taskforce. Officially, all such reports are considered fabrications.

MEN IN BLACK

Despite propaganda to the contrary, there is no single agency which has as its operatives a force who wear black suits and drive old black sedans while investigating alien incursions. However, most of the world's intelligence and counterespionage agencies have at some point had a department or office which covered this subject, and many of their operatives did wear black suits, etc.

Such agencies include, but are not limited to, the following groups:

THE FBI

The Federal Bureau of Intelligence – the FBI – is the United States' national crime fighting and counterespionage organization, which has spent a long time working against what it calls enemy aliens – though this most likely refers simply to humans from other areas (the word 'alien' itself comes from the ancient Latin language, and means 'other').

The Target: Earth

Their two most famous modern-day agents, however, are a pair of unusual characters who devoted their service almost entirely to investigating reports of extraterrestrial activity. The Agency also, along with local law enforcement, receives many reports of alien activity from conscientious citizens every year.

THE CIA

The Central Intelligence Agency is the United States' main overseas intelligence service, and one of their analysts will often turn up in any area where potential alien threats are being reported. Such agents may be put in charge of small military units of four to six troops, but these should pose little threat, as the troops will probably be more distrustful of the agent than alert to your activities.

If you or your forces are equipped with adaptive camouflage, such units are no threat whatsoever.

THE FSB

Along with the Russian Air Force, the KGB has a long history of receiving and investigating reports of alien activity, especially around secret missile bases and launch sites.

Now that they have been renamed the FSB, in the post-Communist version of Russia, they maintain the same old smiling service in both their investigations of crime, terrorism and espionage, as well as in being a repository for reports of alien activity.

Those of you with telepathic or psychokinetic ability might be interested to know that, some decades ago, the then-KGB used to have a lab devoted to such abilities on the seventh floor of their headquarters at Dzerzhinsky Square in Moscow. If the lab is still active, you may find it useful, or a threat to be eliminated first, depending on the context.

DI55

In Britain, reports of alien activity were traditionally handled not by spy agencies like MI5 or MI6, but by DI55, a branch of the Royal Air Force's Air Technical Investigation Branch, which otherwise was more commonly used by the Ministry of Defence for investigating accidents and crashes of their planes.

The Ministry had a UFO office in London, while DI55 itself investigated reports made by the military, and radar detections of alien activity, through their radar base at Rudloe Manor.

The alien investigation branch has, of course, been shut down as part of an economic austerity programme, and should therefore pose no threat.

STUDIOS

Many people on Earth believe that the prevalence of fictional artworks involving alien invasions of Earth is a possible sign that the corporations creating these works know that the Earth is about to be invaded – or at least make contact with extraterrestrial life – and are using a sort of psychological programming to prepare the human population for the revelation of this fact.

If this is true, it wouldn't be much of a stretch from there to the idea that a studio corporation might itself be a cover for monitoring alien activity, so that the populace could be further educated or warned. This would at first make such studios a logical target, but see also the section on 'Controlling Humans'.

AMATEURS

For all that there are various militaries, intelligence services, and law enforcement organizations who may all take an interest in your activities, you must not forget that not all resistance groups or threats to your operations will be governmental or official – or even professional.

There will always be those – often younger humans who have yet to have the blinkers installed that will blind them to the universe around them and make them focus on what their leaders want them to do to maintain the status quo – who will take it upon themselves to notice and interfere in your activities.

Some may do it because they wish to exploit your arrival to leave the planet themselves, while others are acting as some kind of vigilantes. Nevertheless, whether they are a group of friends travelling around in a van with their dog, or former government employees with nothing better to do because they live in Wales, these will be the most unpredictable attempts at defence.

ATTACKING THE EARTH

There are several different kinds of actions that come under the general meaning of 'attacking' the Earth – or any other planet, for that matter. The obvious inference is a straightforward invasion, to take over the planet in order to either rule it or exploit its resources.

However, an attack could also be mounted with the intent of either wiping out civilizations or life forms existing there or even destroying the planet itself. The type of attack you intend to make will depend on your ultimate purpose in targeting the Earth. If you're looking for a suitable environment in which to live and expand your influence, then invasion – or possibly terraforming – is your best bet. If you want to prevent others from exploiting the planet, then you may wish to destroy it entirely. This may also be the case if you consider the existence of the planet itself a danger to you, or if it is in the way of your logistical plans.

There have been suggestions on Earth over the years that offworld civilizations might be sufficiently concerned at the development of such quaint technologies as nuclear weapons, as to decide that these weapons are a threat even over interstellar distances. A threat has to be eliminated, and if your species believes that the Earth is a direct threat, then you will want, rightly, to eliminate that threat. You will want to destroy the Earth and humanity.

Who doesn't, after all?

THERE'S SUPPOSED TO BE A KABOOM!

There is a temptation, when thinking of destroying a planet or its population, to design a weapon capable of not just eliminating the enemy life form(s), but of completely destroying the physical body of the planet itself. Blowing stuff up is always satisfying.

The most famous example in terrestrial media is the Death Star in *Star Wars*, an armoured space station the size of a small moon, which is armed with a gigantic projected energy weapon capable of causing an entire planet to physically explode. (The means of this explosion is never quite explained, but may perhaps be the result of heating the interior core beyond the capacity of the rocky crust to contain the gases and pressures thus generated.)

In other propaganda films made on Earth, a similar effect has been achieved by means of explosives introduced to the core via mining shafts, the use of the Illudium PU-36 explosive space modulator, by the sheer overwhelming firepower of massed fleets of capital ships' weaponries, or by stellar construction equipment. This isn't as daft as it sounds, when you consider that the gravity well of a planet or star system will affect the travel of particles and waves through it.

In at least one piece of literature, an arrangement of black holes was said to have been used as a barrel to fire projectile suns and planets at target worlds, which is really taking things to unnecessary excess.

Although this temptation for physical deconstruction is quite natural and exciting, your strategic planners and those who determine your military doctrine should be sure to consider all of the information available, before deciding upon the best means to eliminate a planet from the battlefield entirely, should it be necessary or desirable to do so. This is a big decision to make, not just ethically and morally, but in terms of the sheer amount of energy and action required to execute such a massive change to the local order of things.

Assuming you have ascertained the desire and/or certainty to take the Earth out of the equation entirely, rather than to conquer it, you must decide whether to actually destroy its physical form, sterilize the planet so that whatever was problematic there no longer exists, or conduct the extinction of only selected life forms and/or civilizations.

We Will Destroy Your Planet

The use of so-called 'berserker' devices falls under this type of attack, and some thought has been given to the concept on Earth.

A berserker would be an automated probe which sends out a signal to a planet it visits, to test whether life there has achieved a specific level of sentience and/or technological development. If the berserker device receives a reply (and, naturally, the signal should be offering something that the planetary population would want to reply to), it detonates, destroying the planet. Depending on the design, the berserker may destroy the planet by other means than self-destruction – perhaps returning to the Death Star/giant energy weapon, but the principle is the same.

While it is certainly impressive, and a mark of your power and technological development and ingenuity, to physically reduce a planet to rubble, destroying the Earth completely will undoubtedly be beyond the technology of many spacefaring species.

Planets are, to put it bluntly, built to last, and the Earth is no exception.

To be completely blown apart, in the manner of a victim of the Death Star, or Vulcan in 2009's *Star Trek* reboot, the Earth would have to suffer the release of an incredible amount of energy – basically equivalent to the amount of all the potential energy bound up within its atomic structure. For those with a numerical bent, this is something on the order of 2.25 x 10 to the power of 32 joules. That's billions of times the amount of energy released in any nuclear explosion ever detonated on Earth. Specifically, it would take 50 billion times as much energy – and not a mere 20 nukes as Martha Jones seemed to think in the *Dr Who* episode 'Journey's End'.

In fact, the energy requirement is equivalent to crashing a celestial body with at least 60% of the Earth's mass into the planet, at a velocity at least equal to the Earth's own escape velocity, which is roughly 23,500 miles per hour.

Attacking The Earth

That's such a massive energy requirement that the Moon itself falling out of the sky and crashing into the Earth still wouldn't be enough of an impact to do anything like the required amount of damage (as the mass of the Moon is only about 1/85th the mass of the Earth). The obvious thought would be that a larger impactor would be more likely to fulfil the requirements, and it's natural to wonder if something closer to the size and mass of Mars would be good enough to do the job.

It wouldn't. In fact, not only will Mars falling into the Earth not create the required level of physical destruction – those energy requirements are, really, literally, astronomical – but, believe it or not, this has already happened, and the Earth is still here.

Those of you with time travel capability can confirm or deny this for yourselves, but the Moon is now thought to have been created when an object the size of Mars, and with about 10% of the Earth's mass, hit the still-forming Earth four and a half billion years ago and smashed it apart. Even this wasn't enough energy to permanently sunder the planet, which re-formed under its own gravitational influence over time.

That said, if you could fire present-day Mars (which has a mass of 11% that of the Earth) into the Earth at a speed about six times greater than escape velocity – 140,000 miles per hour should be right – the velocity should make up for the difference in mass, and successfully destroy both planets.

Venus, however, the next planet sunwards from Earth, has approximately 80% the mass of the Earth, and so absolutely would do the job of pulverizing the Earth to rubble, if crashed into the Earth even at escape velocity. So, what else can we use to blow up the Earth?

Antimatter, and in particular antimatter bombs, are often considered a good option, as matter and antimatter brought into contact with each other will mutually annihilate, releasing almost 100% of the energy stored in the atomic structure of both.

This efficiency of mass-energy conversion is usually focussed upon by people who think of it to the exclusion of how to actually achieve it, however. You may be wondering how much antimatter would be required to release the Earth's 2.25x10 to the power of 32 of energy. It's a lot. In fact, you would need 1,246,400,000,000 tonnes of antimatter. Well, actually, you'd need a lot more even than that, because a lot of that energy would be lost in heat and light and so on, rather than in true mass-energy conversion of planetary material. So you can consider the 1.244 trillion tons as the bare minimum, or a starting point.

Letting loose a few anti-atoms, or even a handful of antimatter, is *not* going to get you your Earth-shattering kaboom.

EXTERMINATE!

Since physically destroying the entire structure of the Earth is such a wastefully resource-intensive business, and in fact unlikely to succeed anyway, sterilizing the planet of all life forms is a more practicable alternative in most cases (with the obvious exceptions of the planet being a physical obstruction of some kind, perhaps to the route of a hyperspatial bypass).

There are many reasons why you may intend to completely sterilize the planet, but enabling the stripping of it for resources is perhaps the most likely. Native life forms have a tendency to get in the way of major planetary mining operations, and unless you have a particular need for the use of slave labourers to carry the rocks around, it's generally more convenient to not have the risk of resistance.

Unfortunately, wiping out absolutely all life on Earth – regardless of how fragile its position is, when placed in the context of the infinite void and darkness of space – is also actually a more difficult proposition than you might think. Terrestrial life has proven itself to be remarkably hardy at times. The Earth has suffered numerous large-scale natural extinction-level events over the span of its existence, and none have ever quite completely eliminated life from the planet.

The most well known (to the dominant native life form) extinction event is the so-called K/T impact at the changeover between the Cretaceous and Tertiary geological eras, 65 million years ago. (No, Cretaceous doesn't start with a K, despite the acronym.) This event wiped out around 70% of all species, of all types and forms of life, extant at the time. The most destructive extinction event in the planetary history was 251 million years ago, when the Permian–Triassic extinction eliminated a massive 95% of the species on the planet.

The K/T impact is thought by many of Earth's scientists to have been caused by an 8-mile wide (some say 6 miles, others 9) asteroid 65 million years ago, and left a crater 110 miles wide at what is Chicxulub, in the Yucatan Peninsula. Other scientists believe a structure called the Shiva crater, off the east coast of India, indicates a much larger impact, which could have caused this mass extinction. (The Shiva crater is 370 miles by 250, suggesting an impactor 25 miles wide. It's possible that both impacts could have resulted from the break-up of a single larger body.)

Not all Earth's scientists agree that either of these was responsible for the extinction of the dinosaurs. Some believe that other factors, such as volcanic activity, climate change, or simple overpopulation leading to an inadequacy of food supplies were as much responsible. There is also much debate over whether the Shiva crater is in fact an impact crater, or a product of natural geomorphology.

In any case, the use of such large impactors proves not to be as reliable as one might expect, when it comes to genocide.

We Will Destroy Your Planet

Altogether, 25% of species did survive (including the likes of sharks, crocodilians, Coelacanths, and so on), and none of them had constructed reinforced underground bunkers, which some humans have done over the years as protection in the event of nuclear war.

If the goal is to wipe out all terrestrial species, it would be more effective to alter the chemical makeup of the atmosphere and oceans, rendering them inimical to carbon-based life. This too may leave a certain amount of survivors, however, as there are various smaller single-cell life forms the likes of which are capable of surviving even in such altered circumstances. For example, there are water bears, and organisms that live around the vents of so-called 'black smokers' deep under the ocean, at crushing pressures and high temperatures.

No such creatures are sophisticated or likely to offer resistance to invasion, of course, but there is always the theoretical chance that they could evolve to threaten you at some future date. And it's frustrating to be unable to complete a set.

To put this into perspective, 99.9% of all the species that have ever existed in Earth's history are now extinct, and yet there are still literally millions of species, from sentient space travellers to single-celled virii, and from avian species that soar in the skies, to strange multi-cellular creatures that can only live in the areas around ocean-bottom vents that leak heat from the Earth's core. Life on the planet is tenacious in the extreme, and some of it always survives somewhere, no matter what the extinction event.

It would, therefore, be something of a challenge to destroy absolutely all life on the planet, as anything guaranteed to do so – and this would have to be on the order of a massive solar event, such as the Sun swelling into a red giant, and burning the planet to the extent of the sea and atmosphere burning off into space – would be likely to render the structure of the planet unsuitable for the acquisition of resources. If such a

Attacking The Earth

planet was ideal for your purposes, you perhaps would have been better off finding a world in such a position to begin with, rather than expending the energy required to have the Earth reach such a state.

Biological warfare would be a much better option, especially if the goal is merely to wipe out humanity and leave the rest of the biosphere intact for use and exploitation. A biological pathogen could be engineered to be inimical to the human species, and other species you want rid of, without harming yourself. Pathogens that would affect humanity are unlikely to affect any invading species, and vice-versa. Humanity has, of course, made it easier to spread a suitably lethal pandemic globally, by instituting a global transport network of pressurized aerial vehicles.

There would undoubtedly be survivors in isolated areas – even with a long-lasting airborne pathogen, the weather patterns of the winds could allow areas of the planet to remain uncontaminated – so you would then have to hunt down and eliminate them, by whatever means.

It is theoretically possible that a virus genetically engineered to be inimical to all carbon-based life forms could eventually accomplish the task, but the likelihood of those pockets of life existing out of contact with each other make it unlikely that true 100% infection could ever be achieved.

The extent of life remaining might well be reduced to something as simple as single-celled organisms, or non-sentient creatures existing in the depths of the oceans, but they would still be there as a symbol of your failure, and may have the potential to evolve into something more threatening later. They would also, of course, be far harder to track down, and detect and eliminate, than groups of large mammals. That being said, it would still be your best way of trying for the complete extinction of life.

DESTROY ALL HUMANS!

If wiping out the dominant species, humanity, will suffice for your purposes, then matters become far more practicable. There are many good reasons for taking out the dominant species on Earth before you invade, but the most important one is to prevent the danger of active resistance. There is a simple way of almost certainly wiping out humanity and so guaranteeing total lack of resistance while you carry out your chosen operations on the planet.

That way has already been touched upon in earlier sections: the use of large natural impactors against the planetary surface. Or, to put it another way, asteroid bombardment. The use of asteroid bombardment will guarantee not just large-scale elimination of population centres, but also changes to the climate of the planet, rendering it uninhabitable by humans. Changing the atmosphere and climate can also be achieved by planetary engineering, or terraforming, as it's called on Earth, but that is a technique more useful for long-term planning than as warfare, and will be addressed in the chapter on 'Living On Earth'.

METEOR BOMBARDMENT

Having mentioned asteroid impacts, it's time to look at meteor bombardment as a general tactic in assaulting the planet. Bear in mind that even if you don't intend to destroy the Earth or to wipe out humanity, it is still necessary to eliminate local surface defences prior to invasion, and meteor bombardment is an excellent tactic for this.

The golden rule with this form of warfare is to make sure not to use unnecessary excess energy in delivering these natural warheads to their targets. Such adaptation of natural weaponry has been used in a few dramas over the years.

Attacking The Earth

Where the forces depicted in these dramas have tended to go wrong is in using technology such as mass drivers – using arrays of magnetic linear accelerators to accelerate a metallic mass such as an iron-dense asteroid – to launch chunks of space rock at target planets. For example, in the TV series *Babylon 5*, the Centauri use mass drivers built into their capital warships to pummel the planet Narn with meteors, turning the whole globe into a ruined dustbowl.

This proved three things: 1) space superiority is effective in besieging a planet from orbit; 2) bombardment with meteors really will do plenty of damage to a planet's biosphere, and 3) the Centauri are idiots with more money (or resources) than sense.

Why are they idiots? Because they had no need to build ships that use a (probably quite high) percentage of their power to accelerate lumps of rock, so long as the target planet has a gravity well. As all planets do.

The mass driver isn't that new an idea; they were first thought of as a weapon by Robert A. Heinlein in his 1966 novel *The Moon is a Harsh Mistress*. In the book, the population of a Lunar mining colony wants to secede from being ruled by the authorities on Earth, and, as part of their campaign, use a linear accelerate built in the vicinity of the Mare Undarum to launch rocks at cities on Earth.

What seems to have been forgotten by later thinkers on the matter of meteoric bombardment is that the Loonies (as the rebels are referred to in the book) need to accelerate their rocky payloads to the Moon's escape velocity (5,400 miles per hour) in order to get them off the Moon and heading towards Earth. A rock already placed into the gravity well may need a nudge to get it on course to impact with a particular point on the surface, but it won't need anything like the amount of energy required to impart an escape velocity from a decent-sized body.

From the Centauri point of view in *Babylon 5*, conducting a general bombardment of the surface as a whole, giving the rock a good shove out the airlock, would have done the job.

Also, because of the simple fact of Newtonian physics – every reaction has an equal but opposite reaction – a spacecraft-mounted mass driver would actually function better as an engine than as a weapon. It is, after all, exactly how rockets work. There's a gorgeous visual image used in the title sequences of the later *Babylon 5* seasons showing one of the main characters standing at a window, in which is reflected the image of rocks being launched from his ship's mass drivers. Sadly, it does not show the ship suddenly tumbling backwards away from us, which is what should actually have happened next.

In short, do not try using ship-mounted mass drivers to launch your asteroid bombardment. Let gravity do the work; it's cheaper, easier, and more effective.

This approach is more rarely seen in drama and literature, but is not entirely unknown. Oddly, one of the best examples is in the otherwise comedic film *Iron Sky*, which is about a group of escaped Nazis who have been hiding out in a Lunar base for decades, who then return to try conquering the Earth. At one point their flying saucers are seen to tow big rocks to release into the Earth's gravity well while the ships themselves peel away. This is, in fact, the far more sensible and energy-efficient way to do it.

If merely thinning out the surviving populace will suffice for your purposes, you should take note that disease will be rife among most of the animal species after the asteroid bombardment, whether you help it along by introducing suitable pathogens or not.

The large numbers of unburied dead and lack of food and clean water resulting after such a disaster will mean harmful bacteria will spread like wildfire through the surviving population. This is well worth exploiting, so long as you have no need of strong captives, as it will further lessen the likelihood and ability of any resistance to your arrival and your plans.

Alternatively, you can always pose as benefactors, curing the pandemic, in the hope of gaining human trust. This may be a worthwhile tactic if you are relatively few in number and require an amount of goodwill and help from the population.

It goes without saying, of course, that if you are coming to Earth by means other than starships, then asteroid bombardment will not be an available option. Also, if you are coming from a parallel Earth or from a different period in the planet's history, and are human yourself, then using a global pandemic as an option is definitely not a wise course of action, due to the risk of some of your forces carrying the pathogen back to your time/dimension and wiping out that population also. At the very least, you will have to make sure all your own populace is inoculated against the chosen disease.

In that instance, your best option for wiping out the native population may simply be to gain access to the Earth's national nuclear launch codes, and trigger a global nuclear war. You will have to wait some considerable time afterwards, however, for the radiation levels to settle to a point at which you can safely move in and begin full operations or settlement.

THE [INSERT YOUR NAME HERE] INVASION OF EARTH

Most hostile extraterrestrial interest in the Earth will be in the form of planned invasion and takeover, though the base motive behind that intention will, of course, vary. Whether it's a desire for living space, the planet's chemical resources, strategic position, livestock, or just because it's fun to conquer a planet and gives your military something to do, there are a number of things you must do correctly.

DO YOUR RESEARCH

Before embarking on any military campaign, you must gather information. The successful interplanetary conqueror will always be the one who has gathered every possible piece of knowledge and calculated every possible eventuality. Conquests are made in the research and planning stage, not in the running around screaming 'it's game over, man,' stage. It's admittedly a truism that no battle plan ever survives first contact with the enemy, but this is why you must be prepared with alternate plans in advance.

Even on Earth, the wisdom holds true that the warrior who knows both the enemy and themselves will always win; the warrior who knows themselves but not the enemy will win and lose equally; and the warrior who knows neither really ought to give up and get a civilian day job.

So, knowing your enemy – in this case human society – is an absolute must. If you are coming from a parallel world, you may already know much of what you need, but not everything; there will always be differences, and even if not, you'll still be dealing with other nations, whose strategy and tactics are secret to you even in your own identical world. If you're coming from the past, you will have records and histories, but these are written by the victors, and usually with a political slant, so may be unreliable. It will always be better to infiltrate and investigate yourself – and at least you will have the advantage of being able to pass for a local with authority.

If you're an extraterrestrial coming by a means – such as a wormhole or matter-transmission beam – that will have you arrive directly on the surface, you will also have to do your research by means of either electronic intelligence gathering (tapping data and communications) or infiltration. If you are unable to infiltrate by stealth, you can always try controlling authorized humans by means of telepathy or even simple bribery. Use of robots and drones is also advised, especially if they can be camouflaged as humans or as other acceptable Earth species that will not arouse suspicion.

Starship crews, however, have the best possible view. Literally. The Earth can be sampled in total from orbit, by all possible kinds of scanners and cameras and sensors. It is a simple matter to map the entire surface, both in the visual spectrum of light for your species, and internally by mass spectrometry, radar, gravitometry, and so on. Using the appropriate sensors from orbit will give you a total picture of the Earth from core to outer atmosphere, as well as showing you where humanity has its military strongpoints, where resource deposits are, and the distribution of life forms. You will also be able to track vehicle movement, and eavesdrop on all electronic communications and broadcasts. Be aware, though, that the Earth has hundreds of languages, and you will need to be able to decode them. (Despite this, you will find from the broadcasts that humans seem to think that all other planets share one single language.)

A warning: *Do* do your research, but be aware of the limitations of your information. Military secrets, generally, are considered to be the shortest-lived as well as the most valuable, but it's less often recognized that simple information is also extremely short-lived in a military context.

As with any commander, you must make sure that your information is as precise and up to date as possible. It must be accurate, and it must be correct for the time of your attack. This brings a bit of a paradox, because, on the one hand you will want to be prepared well in advance with all of the information you need, but that information must also be current at the latest possible moment before conquest. There's no point in knowing where all the defences are before you take off, if they've moved by the time you arrive.

As you can imagine, this is especially problematic for those of you crossing the void in normal space, or even at relativistic speed. If it takes you years to reach the Earth, then the information you have gathered absolutely will be out of date by the time you arrive, unless you have some kind of time travel capability that allows you to move back through time as you cross space, in order to arrive at a point at which your information is current and correct.

It would make more sense, therefore, to conduct your reconnaissance and intelligence-gathering from a forward base – perhaps on the Moon or Mars, or at one of the LaGrange points in the Earth-Sun or Earth-Moon system – so that you can prepare to launch your attack from there.

PREPARE THE GROUNDWORK

There are several stages to an invasion of a territory, regardless of the scale or purpose of the conflict. Broadly speaking, defences and warning systems must be rendered ineffective – or at least disrupted – before the following sequence can occur: entering the target territory, establishing secure beachheads which can be linked together to form a stable controlled area for the later reception of reinforcements and supplies, eliminating military resistance in surrounding territory, and consolidating control of suppressed territory.

In Earth's history, invasions have been conducted both by crossing land borders, by landing troops at the coast from maritime ships, and by airborne transport of parachute troops. The most effective landing method for you will depend on your means of transport, and how you arrive at Earth. There is no defensive shielding, so, in order of importance, you will need to deal with the following layers of national defences across most of the planet:

First off, you will need to be sure to neutralize defensive forces on the ground, and eliminate air defences that may intercept your re-entry vehicles. Depending upon how much of the planetary society you want to preserve for whatever

reason, your means of dealing with native forces will differ.

If your intent is to preserve and exploit humanity (as slaves, food, or whatever), you will need to be precise in your opening bombardment. Laser strikes from orbit, precision-guided missiles with conventional or antimatter warheads, or low-yield tactical nuclear weapons are all viable options for taking out military bases, command and control centres, and so on.

If you have no interest in preserving the native population, and simply want the planet for its mineral resources or as a strategic garrison, then 20 or so mile-wide asteroids directed to impact on low-lying plains and population centres will eliminate all practical resistance in advance, and save you a lot of time, effort, and logistics in holding the planet later.

COMMUNICATIONS NETWORKS

It will greatly reduce local forces' ability to organize and co-ordinate their resistance if you can shut down as close to all terrestrial communications as possible. Doing so will prevent commanders from issuing orders, field units from making situation reports, governments from executing policy, military units from being directed to where your forces are, and so much more besides.

The silence between the authorities and their populations will also have the effect of leaving the populations confused and frightened. They will therefore be more concerned with panicking over their lack of knowledge than resisting your invasion. Similarly, the authorities, especially in urban areas and near political control centres, will have to divert manpower to police their own populations, thus reducing their numbers available to be deployed to the front lines and bridgehead areas where you will be landing.

Fortunately, advances in technology on Earth have actually made this task simpler, rather than more difficult. A couple of decades ago, bringing down the human communications networks would require eliminating exchange buildings filled with electromechanical technology across the globe. Every country and alliance would have to be targeted separately, as they all have separate technical set-ups and political systems, as well as different chains of command.

Currently, however, Earth has digital communications enabled by microwave transmissions, along with wireless frequencies, and almost all communications devices use microelectronic technology. All of which is vulnerable to the whims of electromagnetism. A strong enough electromagnetic pulse in or near the Earth's atmosphere will render all such devices over a wide area completely useless, preventing any signal transmission. In the local parlance, the technology would be 'bricked' – in other words as electronically active as a baked lump of clay.

A sufficiently strong EMP might well be able to completely inhibit all such devices across the planet, rendering it radio-dark, and thus preventing any signal communication before your landings. The means to produce such a large EMP are varied, both in natural and artificial means.

The largest and most devastating form of EMP would be a naturally generated gamma-ray burst, either from a stellar event such as a supernova, or from a suitable large solar flare event. Solar weather would have the best chance of blanketing the entire planet with charged protons and electrons capable of taking out vital transformers, satellites, and so on. The US and UK governments, two nations which you will certainly come into contact and conflict with, have both recently produced reports acknowledging that a serious Solar energy event could knock out much of the planet's power and communications systems for weeks, and possibly up to a year.

The best way to engineer a solar coronal mass ejection, which would send a storm of particles out towards the Earth, would be to generate two massive electromagnetic fields over a sunspot – a darker area in the Sun's upper atmosphere – and let the protons and electrons build up into a loop of plasma between the fields, which would then rise in temperature well beyond the Sun's coronal temperature. When the protons and electrons in this plasma reach a terminal velocity of 900,000 mph they join the solar wind. If the particles in the plasma reach the Sun's escape velocity of 1,390,500 mph or above, they can burst into a solar flare or even a full coronal mass ejection – a blast of plasma shot into space like some kind of weapon.

When this plasma hits the Earth's magnetosphere, it actually deforms the Earth's magnetic field, even changing the reactions of compass needles. It also can induce large electrical ground currents in the conductive iron of the Earth itself. This sort of magnetic storm causes aurorae in the atmosphere, damages satellites – or, indeed, visiting and unshielded starships, so be careful about trying this – in orbit, and, if strong enough, will disrupt global communications and wreck electrical and electronic equipment on the surface or in the atmosphere.

However, if your ship is capable of travelling across interstellar distances, and/or travelling faster than light or through hyperspace, it should be capable of generating a suitable orbital EMP pulse. After all, even humanity can do that, which is handy if you're arriving by wormhole, time travel or dimensional rift, and want to use an EMP to knock out planetary communications. All you will need are some nuclear weapons.

It is well known on Earth that nuclear weapons cause an electromagnetic pulse as a first side effect of the detonation of a fission device. For the widest of coverage of the EMP effect, a detonation at an altitude of 250 miles above sea level is recommended. The area affected by the EMP effect will be a roughly U-shaped area, with 60–70% of the effect being on the equatorial side of the detonation. (That is to say, EMPs triggered in the northern hemisphere will mostly affect areas southward of the detonation area, and those triggered in the southern hemisphere will more affect areas northward of the detonation point.)

The amount of energy radiated will vary according to both the altitude of the detonation and the geographical location. The Earth's magnetic field is stronger over land masses and closer to the poles. If identical EMP devices were detonated over both the equatorial Pacific Ocean and the cities of the Eastern Seaboard of the United States, the EMP over those American cities would be at least five times stronger.

Use of nuclear warheads to knock out communications over large areas of land is, therefore, not an impractical solution to the planetary communications network. That said, if you're going to use nuclear warheads you may as well use them strategically to destroy military centres, population centres, and so on while you're at it, and leave the EMP effect just as a side effect.

Humanity has known about the dangers and effects of EMP for decades, however, and some military infrastructures have their electrical and electronic devices shielded against the effect. Interestingly, as the local geopolitical situation on Earth has drifted away from the threat of an exchange of nuclear warheads, and towards lower-key guerrilla actions, the habit of shielding new equipment against EMP has slipped in many of Earth's militaries. Not only that, but more modern technology is more fragile, and microcircuits are less robust than the thick copper wiring and cables of the past, so, with these two changes in circumstance combined, much of the Earth's technology today is actually more vulnerable to EMP than it was at earlier stages of development.

This, of course, is entirely to your advantage.

COMMAND AND CONTROL CENTRES

As the Earth is still not yet a unified society, each of its nation-states has its own militaries with their own command and control centres. These centres are, however, devoted to running operations concerned with other terrestrial nation-states, rather than with planetary defence.

Nevertheless, they will be used to co-ordinate any defence against an assault on the planet as a whole, though it is unlikely that – at least in the early stages of such a campaign – the militaries of rival nations would share their command structures against the common foe.

Many of the main command and control centres belonging to the major military powers are well sheltered, safely ensconced in environs – natural or artificial – proofed against nuclear warheads. In some cases these are specially designed and constructed to be proofed against nuclear strikes, while others are built under natural defences such as mountains, which were already strong enough to withstand such attacks.

Most notably, NORAD and the US Air Force's Space Command (the clue as to why this base is important is in the latter's name) are settled beneath Cheyenne Mountain in Colorado. This is where, in the *Stargate* series of media, the Stargate itself is housed, and the location from which units of Earth soldiers make their forays to other planets. As far as is known, this is still fiction, but you will probably have detected the transmissions on the way to Earth and so be wary of this facility.

Meteor bombardment is, again, going to be the best way to deal with such fortified control centres. Anything over a hundred yards or so across should deal with any underground facility, mountains above them notwithstanding.

Attacks not from space will have to use other means, and this will be tricky for those time travellers and dimension-jumpers relying on the Earth's own weapons to do the job, since, as stated, these facilities tend to be hardened against nuclear blasts. Infiltration and sabotage will be the best options for such invaders.

Those of you with the use of wormholes or teleportation, on the other hand, can have fun with materializing tactical nuclear warheads *inside* the nuke-proof fortifications and the inevitable devastating results.

MISSILE LAUNCH SITES

This category of target is probably the most obvious one. Since the Earth only has rockets and missiles as weapons usable against spaceborne enemies, removing them must be a priority for any spaceborne assault.

Attacking The Earth

Although there are large launch sites for manned space missions, in both the Western and Eastern hemispheres, most military missile sites are much smaller, more likely to be hidden, and, indeed, often mobile. This means that asteroid bombardment is less likely to be effective. A suitable EMP burst, as already discussed, will render launch protocols ineffective. While the missile launch systems are down, it is recommended that you use your own missiles with tactical nuclear warheads (if you have them), energy weapons, or atmospheric attack craft to strafe or bomb such sites as they are detected.

Non-spaceborne attackers may not need to specifically target these sites, as the missiles will be less of a threat to materialization or reintegration from a wormhole, or to ground troops. Nevertheless, it's still a wise move to plan for dealing with them, so that they can't be used to launch strikes against you on the surface, or to launch satellites that would help the native population with their global campaign against you. To that end, sabotage, or outright commando raids are all on the table as options.

AIRCRAFT CARRIERS

The most important – and dangerous, even to an assault from offworld or from other dimensions or eras – element of Earth's current defensive capability is the capital warship known as the aircraft carrier.

This, obviously, is a large vessel capable of transporting, launching and recovering warplanes. These leviathans are therefore the vital backbone of the ability of Earth's larger militaries to project their force and effectiveness to any part of the planet. In essence the aircraft carrier is a mobile military base, which is therefore slightly harder to target and remove than a structure on land. It is vital, however, that you do, as the aircraft carrier can manoeuvre closer to your landing zones or wormhole exits, and deploy warplanes quickly to intercept landing craft during their descent through the atmosphere, or to attack your forces on the surface.

Currently, despite some of the visual footage you may have intercepted that has been broadcast from the planet, all such carriers are in fact surface-based ships, confined to the 70% of the Earth's surface that is ocean. There are, as yet, no aerial carrier vessels. This has not always been the case, oddly enough. Some 80 years ago, nations such as the United States and Germany did toy with the idea of mounting deployable and recoverable interceptor aircraft aboard dirigible airships. Such a carrier would be able to move anywhere in the Earth's atmosphere in attempts to evade detection and approach enemy targets.

In reality, however, it turned out that such dirigible motherships were in fact slow, difficult to mount defensive weapons aboard, and prone to exploding and crashing on their own. As better military aircraft, aircraft carriers, and in-flight refuelling techniques were developed, the aerial carrier idea was allowed to fade.

AIRBASES

With mobile carrier ships eliminated, you would be best advised to deal with airbases on land surfaces.

Obviously these bases are fixed installations, and so cannot move in order to escape detection and destruction, but any installation capable of launching atmospheric craft that can attack your landing vessels or ground forces is a priority threat that must be dealt with.

Depending on your available resources and intentions for the local life forms and surrounding environs, you can use any method you like for the destruction of such bases, up to and including the use of nuclear warheads, meteor bombardment, or antimatter warheads. It's worth noting, however, that humanity as yet has no antigravity technology available for their warplanes. This means that, with a few exceptions, their interceptors must accelerate down a paved runway in order to take off. Such runways are easily disabled by blasting craters into them, or blocking them with wreckage, which leaves the interceptors useless, and negates the necessity to waste heavier weapons on trying to break through to more heavily fortified hangars and storage areas.

The exception to this rule is Changchu'an-ni Airbase, in North Korea. This is the world's only (known) *entirely* underground airbase, runways included. This suggests that either a) the North Koreans have some form of advanced technology that allows their planes to phase through solid matter, making them the most dangerous interceptors the Earth has to offer, or b) the North Koreans have a really strange attitude to military architecture, but in any case this is one airbase you'll probably have to drop a meteor on, if you want to make a clean sweep of the airfields.

OTHER MILITARY BASES

Other types of military bases – frontline firebases, barracks, training grounds, fuel depots, etc – can be dealt with as you see fit. The important thing, however, is to be certain not to leave any resistance operational within your landing areas or bridgeheads, or behind the front lines of your expansion.

Any bases within your sphere of influence will have to be rendered harmless, by being destroyed or taken over. Otherwise, they risk being centres for organized resistance within your area, and able to attack the flanks of your expansion. This would be highly problematic, and endanger your consolidation of captured ground. Do not allow this.

YOU MAY START YOUR LANDING

Clearly, if you are invading from starships, your strategy will be most similar to the 20th century's use of airborne troops. The advantage to landing your forces from above – as opposed to on coastline or across land borders – is that you are not restricted to those areas on which defences are strongest. Obviously any civilization will put its strongest defences on the borders and the coasts, but from above you can land your troops absolutely anywhere. Obviously you have brought enough troops to hold at least a couple of waves in reserve after you commit your first wave. Never, ever, commit your entire force to a single operation, or even the invasion of a single planet.

The freedom to choose your landing sites at will is doubly advantageous if you have been able to destroy or otherwise negate the target's military power and infrastructure in advance. If you haven't managed this, then your strategy must include picking suitable landing zones that will meet the balance of allowing you to establish bridgeheads in vital areas quickly, while maximizing the response time from local forces.

Pro-tip: since you can monitor transmissions around the Earth from orbit, you should be able to determine which types of signals and media are used by humans, which are even known to humans, and by extension, which are unknown. You should therefore make sure to keep any communications between your forces to those signals and frequencies, which will not be detected or interpreted on Earth.

If you are operating to a particular time schedule, make sure to synchronize your timekeeping devices before you reach the Earth, and work to a plan, rather than openly transmitting obvious countdowns or navigational signals to each other. Repeated sequences of signals between vessels prior to an attack should be avoided at all costs, because even

Attacking The Earth

if your code is incomprehensible, the fact that it is a slightly changing repeated sequence will give the game away.

Maintain communications silence, at least as far as Earth's ears are concerned, and your actions will be far more of a successful surprise.

When it comes to actually landing on the physical surface of the planet, it is tempting to choose landing zones that are hidden or camouflaged. Warfare, after all, is so often a matter of deception; appear to want to land in one place, but do so in another, look weak when you're strong, and so on. This is a mistake when landing from orbit, partly due to the velocities involved in picking a precise location, and partly because – unless your landing vehicles are fitted with cloaking devices, or some other form of stealth technology – the landing craft will be visible and detected by radar on their descent.

The important factors for choosing a landing site, therefore – and especially for a major landing of troops in force – are:

1) That the landing area should be physically safe and stable enough to support the type of vessels you're landing

2) That the landing field be over a large enough area to take many troopships and support vessels

3) That there be enough room for ships that overshoot to still arrive within a defensive perimeter

4) That the landing zone be defensible from counterattack by terrestrial forces.

Taking these requirements in order, the first priority is that your landing area be safe. This means that you ought to be looking for a wide-open space which has solid enough ground to support the weight of your landing craft. If you're using craft which can land, debark troops, and then take off again, you will probably want bedrock as close to the surface as possible.

This means you need a flat surface. Not a steep slope, not a place strewn with boulders higher than your undercarriage, and definitely not the middle of a forest. It may look cool to see transport ships descend directly into forest and jungle, but this would in reality lead to their hulls being crumpled and punctured in a most harmful way. Trees may be made of wood, but old trees, full-grown, are surprisingly strong, especially along their long vertical axis. In fact, when an object from space exploded in the skies of Tunguska in 1908, flattening hundreds of square miles of Siberian forest, the trees directly underneath the airburst were the ones still standing (albeit stripped of branches).

You do not want your landing craft to end up impaled on a tree trunk like a cocktail sausage.

This is assuming you wish to land properly at all, of course. If you intend to bring your transports down to *almost* the surface, and have your troops rappel down, or use some form of personal jetpack to descend, or just jump, then you can land them anywhere, regardless of the terrain in the immediate vicinity. However, you will need to establish transport hubs where individuals and materiel can be embarked – troops finishing their tour, injured troops being evacuated for treatment, prisoners, materiel you've captured – you will certainly have to land those vessels in order to embark for ascent.

You may also, for convenience, use disposable capsules designed only for atmospheric entry and impact with the surface. In this case you may prefer to look for regions with relatively deep layers of soil and sand which can absorb the impact, or even look for landing zones in marshy areas or in the oceans.

Be aware, if you are landing at sea, that you will need support craft already on station to recover the incoming troops or materiel, or else will require your incomers to be amphibious. It would also, of course, be possible to deliver submersible amphibious vehicles into the oceans in this way, which would largely avoid the problem of having your landing craft exposed to counterattack from terrestrial military forces after reaching the surface – though they would subsequently be so exposed when reaching land, and coastal regions are more likely to be defended against incursion anyway.

If you are invading through teleportation or wormholes, or from an alternate Earth either in a parallel dimension or a different time zone, by a means involving some form of materialization or physical reintegration at your destination, you will have to be aware of the range of physical variation in the surface of the Earth. Materializing, for example, inside the solid rock of a mountain will put a sudden stop to your invasion plans.

It is acceptable to pick a transference area, which will be concealed from the native forces, though it must still be large enough for your troops and equipment to be mustered for their advance, and also defensible.

It would also advisable to pick a transition region capable of aiding aviation, so that you can bring aircraft through, either on the ground – in which case you'll want a bridgehead site large enough to have a runway built – or in the air, so that aircraft can be flown through.

Once your forces have established a suitable forward base from which to be resupplied and launch missions, you will need to defend that base.

How best to defend these forward bases? One important factor, once humanity's ability to launch air strikes and missile strikes against you has been negated, is to ensure there's clear space around the perimeter in which you can see potential insurgents coming in their attempts to destroy or steal your ships and technology.

Parking in a city centre heliport is a bad idea, no matter how pacified the city, as the rubble and standing walls will provide plenty of cover for approaching enemies (or, indeed, for fleeing prisoners). Plus, of course, the remnants of the buildings will make bad 'footing' for your craft to land neatly on. This is one of many mistakes made by the Daleks, in both the TV and movie versions of *The Dalek Invasion of Earth*.

We Will Destroy Your Planet

The Empire in the *Star Wars* films is just as foolish with their installations. When a shield generator was necessary to project an energy field around their second Death Star (itself a waste of time, effort, and money, of course), from the moon called Endor, they seriously misjudged how it should be done. Building a facility in the dense and huge trees of a forest that is home to a native species capable of organized resistance would be a big mistake.

Dropping a rock a few hundred yards across into the forest would clear it for miles, and allow a far safer installation to be constructed at the centre of the crater thus excavated. This would have had the double advantage of eliminating the problematic natives for miles around, and leaving an open killing ground around the facility, across which any approach could be viewed and dealt with.

It comes back to asteroid bombardment again. When you absolutely, positively need to kill every motherfrakker in the LZ, accept no substitute.

Alternatively, depending on how solidly-built your ships are, take a tip from the human command and control centres and bury them under hills and mountains. This will prove protection against strikes up to and including nuclear weapons.

Those of you not arriving in ships would be advised to follow that protocol also; build bunkers into and under hills, for the same reason. Maintain weapons emplacements and guard posts on the surface above, against encroaching ground forces, and be sure to maintain the high ground. Also be sure to install anti-aircraft systems, either in the form of missiles, automated weapons, or energy weapons. However you arrived, if you have the ability to cloak your ships and facilities, do so. Also always be sure to make use of whatever force shield technology you have.

Once you are firmly settled on the surface of the planet, it will be time to conduct operations, both military and objective-related, on the surface.

REPEAT OFFENDERS

Some species and cultures have attempted to invade the Earth more often than others, if terrestrial fiction is anything to go by.

The most common invaders of the Earth have always been the natives of that belligerent red planet, Mars. Even not counting the different versions of *War of the Worlds*, there have been so many different types of Martians in other books, comics, movies, and games, that there's no question of the natives of Mars being the number one attackers of the Earth. Different authors, artists and filmmakers have ascribed totally different natures, capabilities and motives to the Martians, but their homeworld and desire to conquer the Earth and wrest it from the grip of humanity has long been a constant factor that links almost every interpretation of the natives of Mars.

Runners-up in the table of making the most repeated attempts to conquer the Earth is probably a single race who have graced the world's TV screens many times – the Daleks. Although not every appearance they have made has involved them attacking the Earth directly, they have attempted to conquer and/or destroy the Earth a total of 11 times on screen alone and more often still in audio, comics and novels.

The various cosmic entities of H. P. Lovecraft's Cthulhu mythos have exerted their baleful influence on Earth from distant times and places quite often, but it's debatable as to whether they're truly invaders, as they tend to just influence minds from afar, and usually when humans have made contact with them first.

SURFACE OPERATIONS

Once your landings have been made, and bridgeheads consolidated so that you can reinforce as necessary, you will be able to begin expanding out from these footholds. You will now be looking at moving around through the Earth's different environmental conditions, and seeking out further objectives to be secured.

Whatever your ultimate aim for the planet, you will now have to be able to work and fight on the surface, in the sea, and in the atmosphere. This means you will require vehicles and equipment, and will need to be prepared for a wide variety of climates and varying conditions in the zones of different types of operations to be conducted.

You will also need to be aware of various environmental situations, and not just those related to active resistance by the natives. It's a jungle out there – and desert, ocean, glacier, veldt... You must be prepared to live, thrive, and survive in all of these different types of environment if you are to seal your conquest of the planet.

ENVIRONMENTAL AWARENESS

Before discussing vehicles, you will need to be sure that your forces can withstand the terrestrial environment when outside of any vehicles. You may need pressure suits, if you evolved in a world with a thinner or denser atmosphere, and breathing equipment if the Earth's atmosphere is not conducive to supporting your form of life.

If you have come from a world with a lower gravity, or are adapted to life in microgravity aboard space vessels, you will probably require support structures for your physical form – limbs and spine, if you have them, for example – in order to withstand long periods on the surface of the Earth. Conversely, if you come from a higher gravity planet, you may find that there are degenerative side effects to being in a lower gravity environment for a long time, though you will probably have already discovered and addressed this issue while becoming adjusted to space travel. (But, see also the chapter on 'Looking After Your Humans'.)

Even if you have encountered the issues of physical degeneration in microgravity, do not assume that these factors cannot still affect you on the surface of the Earth, if you originally came from a location with higher gravity. In such an instance, you may be tempted to assume you will be physically stronger than the natives of a lower gravity planet, but this is not necessarily the case, if your physiology is adapted for load-bearing rather than leverage.

Most of the inhabited regions are temperate in nature, neither too hot nor too cold, though even these areas can reach temperatures over between -25C and 35C at the extremes of the seasons.

Humidity, the amount of water vapour suspended in the air, varies wildly according to location, weather, time of year, type and amount of vegetation, topography, and a host of other factors. In general, areas with large amounts of trees

Surface Operations

and rainfall will have high humidity, especially in summer. This is particularly the case in regions around the equator, bounded by the tropics at 23 degrees north and south of the equator. This belt is a side effect of the Earth's axial tilt, resulting in the area within being able to have the Sun directly overhead at least once during the terrestrial year.

Because this band around the planet has the most direct sunlight, it is home to both the most humid forested areas, and the hottest deserts. On Earth, a desert is defined as an area that receives less than 10 inches of precipitation each year, which, while generally taken to mean arid hot areas, also means that most of the southern polar ice cap qualifies, as it is too cold there for precipitation. These different kinds of deserts have the highest and lowest temperatures on the planet. Within the past hundred years, Death Valley, an area of the Mojave Desert, and the lowest (below sea level) dry land point on the planet, has been known to reach almost 57C, while Antarctica has seen temperatures as low as -89C.

At sea level, on the surface of the Earth, the atmospheric pressure is 14.7 pounds per square inch (psi), called one bar by human scientists (actually, though, it's really 1.013 bar).

This pressure varies both with height above, and depth underwater. Obviously the increase in pressure underwater is more noticeable because water is denser than air, but the differences are considerable at both extremes. Underwater, the pressure increases by one bar for every 33 feet below the surface, due to the sheer mass of the surrounding water. If you have been conducting deep-sea operations, even within pressurized vehicles, you will have to return to the surface in stages. The same applies if you are a native oceanic species that has arrived in the sea and intend to invade the land. This is because, as the pressure decreases, gas bubbles will form in blood and cell structures, which can lead to a most painful death – occasionally by explosion.

Thankfully the differences between sea level and higher altitudes are not quite so extreme.

Above sea level, the atmospheric pressure decreases on average by about 10% for every three thousand feet, though this also varies according to local weather systems that disturb the atmosphere. The lower the pressure drops, the lower the temperature needed for liquids to boil, so if your species has a high liquid content, or dependence, then beware.

In fact, the drop in atmospheric pressure at high altitudes is so acute that even human travellers on foot must stop at different levels to let their biology acclimatize to the lower pressure and different oxygen levels. This, obviously, will be the same for those visitors from parallel Earths or the past or future. Visitors from other planets who require environment suits against the Earth's atmosphere in general should have no problem, as they will be protected anyway. Those who would otherwise be able to withstand the regular surface conditions on Earth should keep pressure suits and portable atmospheric supplies available for use in those areas where the pressure and atmospheric content levels vary.

TAKING THE FIELD

How much actual warfare you engage in during your operations on Earth will depend both on your motivations, and the reaction you receive from the natives. However much fighting you end up doing, the golden rule to remember is that the purpose of warfare is *victory*, not endurance or scale.

When warfare was limited only to units of ground forces on land, and ships at sea, pitched battles of massed units were perfectly normal, as these armies were what decided the rulership of Earth's nations. With the development of aircraft, missiles and drones, this has become less the case, at least for those nations who have such forces. Since you will be coming with superior technology, you should not actually need – unless you're doing it wrong – to engage the enemy in massed naval or infantry battles. Swarms of troops having it out on the open field, while still an attractive idea to certain cloned armies who have no need to concern themselves about casualties, are basically a waste of time, and a sign of bad strategic planning on the part of any invader from orbit.

There will always be the need for smaller-scale engagements, such as commando raids to capture or destroy enemy facilities, but when any army in the field can be eliminated from the air or from space, by bombs, missiles, meteors, energy weapons, or whatever, then there's really no need to land an army of your own to meet the enemy's army. That said, if you have a particular cultural or religious requirement to meet your enemies face to face, then that is your privilege and you can feel free to do so. Naval actions should be similarly unnecessary, of course.

It will be a different matter for those of you arriving from a parallel Earth. In this instance you should simply follow your world's or nation's standard military doctrine for invading a neighbouring society.

Invaders from more advanced time zones, or who have come through teleportation, wormholes, or other non-starship means, will fall somewhere in the middle. It may well be necessary for you to engage terrestrial armies in the field, but your superior technology should enable victory. The rules to remember here are that, aside from having done your research, you should always be deceptive, and warfare has traditionally depended on deception and concealment for victory. Also, your logistics will be of far more importance than those of the native population, or of invaders from orbit. Invaders from orbit can always drop something on the enemy, but you who are confined to the planetary atmosphere cannot, so you *must* be sure that you can bring through enough materiel and reinforcements from your home before you engage the enemy.

We Will Destroy Your Planet

Present-day Earth is a theatre of asymmetric warfare, rather than classical land or sea warfare. This means that the opposing forces are not equal in doctrine or strategy – one side may rely on open strategic bombing and armoured units, while the other concentrates on stealth and infiltration, for example. As a visitor to the planet, it is highly unlikely that you will just happen to be equal in mindset and ability to the human forces opposing you. You will be engaging in asymmetric warfare of one kind or another, and must know in advance which type of warfare you will conduct.

Spaceborne invaders should project their power from above to eliminate enemies at long range, while invaders able to roll massed troops and equipment through a wormhole or dimensional rift can engage in a traditional invasion, and those with little superior technology or backup from home can use stealth and infiltration techniques.

In general, however, all would-be conquerors of the Earth should find themselves in a position of conducting more quick hit-and-run raids to seize or destroy objectives, and policing actions to retain control of captured and pacified areas.

CAMOUFLAGE

As with any other military activity, camouflage is an important part of preparing for and carrying out your invasion. It is always best in military actions to be covert, deceptive, and not seen, unless you have some honour code about being open, or an animal instinct driving your species to be obvious in order to issue challenges.

Assuming neither of those is the case, you should ensure that your forces – both vehicles and warriors – in combat are appropriately camouflaged.

This is easier for any starships you have; even without the need for energy-based cloaking devices, the sheer size of space as compared to any starship makes the ship no more than a speck at most distances, so simply preventing energy leakage from it and painting the hull black is a good way to start. On Earth, and as the individuals or materiel to be camouflaged shrinks in size, things begin to get more difficult. If you have energy-based invisibility shields of any kind, you should of course use them. If not, then there are things you can do instead. Take tips from Earth militaries, by using camouflage paint, and stealth technology.

Vehicles should be painted to blend in with the background environments in which they will be used. If possible, anti-magnetic paint should be used, and any heat exhausts or power systems disguised with heat-absorbent baffles to prevent tracking by heat-seeking sensors. Radar-diffusing paints should also be handy.

As for your troops, they should also be given a means of camouflage. Personal invisibility cloaks are best, but have problematic side effects; if your eyes work the same way as human eyes, they need light to impact the retinas in order to be translated into visual information by the brain. Anything that prevents light from reaching you – such as invisibility – will also prevent this, and so render you blind. Therefore, if you have such cloaks, you will need to equip your forces using them with some other form of sensor to replace their vision.

Otherwise, either their clothing or their outer surfaces (if they do not wear clothing) should be of a drab colour to suit the background of the environment in the combat area, as per human protocols.

GETTING AROUND ON EARTH

Once you have landed your forces on Earth, whether by means of descent from orbit, or arrival through time or across the barriers between dimensions, you will now be faced with the practicalities of mounting your campaign on the Earth's surface.

As you know by now, 70% of the surface is covered with water, but even the remaining 30% is made up of many different types of terrain, and varies wildly in climate and navigability. Once you have boots – or treads, tentacles, or claws – on the ground, you will have to take these different environments into account.

Obviously there are different military doctrines governing actions on land, at sea, and in the air. Your choice(s) of doctrine will depend both upon where you came to Earth from, how you arrived at the planet and your intentions for it, as well as your physical nature and the environmental factors at work.

As species develop civilizations on their home planets, it is natural that their military tendencies begin with the idea of some kind of army on the planetary surface. Whether this be a Wild Hunt of semi-sentient creatures following a naturally hardwired herd instinct, or a professional army of well-trained warriors, the society's overall fighting strategy will have evolved well before the technology for aerospace travel is developed.

As such, every military society will have evolved with the basic setting of amassing troops of peak fitness age, and deploying them to overwhelm and suppress their rival or prey societies and species.

Note that this doesn't literally mean boots on the ground – an avian species will flock where the atmospheric conditions are suited to them, and societies that evolved in liquid environments would perhaps travel in shoals. That said, they would still be fighting bodies confined to the surface conditions of their world, and so those conditions would be ingrained.

Things change when the ability to travel out of the home environment is developed. When a land-based species

develops air power, that will change its need for marching on the ground. Likewise, the shoal of marine life will have to adapt to not being able to move in three dimensions when it rolls onto dry land, and the flock of avians will also find changes when it submerges to explore the oceans, for example. If you are invading the Earth from a parallel world, or from a different time zone, but are otherwise human and native to an Earth, you should already be familiar with the principles addressed in this section. Having developed in a situation comparable to that which is known today, you will, of course, have experienced a history of evolving infantry and naval warfare at the very least.

We Will Destroy Your Planet

Those of you who have crossed the stars, on the other hand, may have evolved in a completely different biosphere, or one with fewer geological, climatological, or environmental variances. In that case – and especially if this is your first invasion of a planet other than your own – you would be more advised to pay attention to the following.

FIELDS OF BATTLE

Because the Earth's surface environments vary so much, you will need specialist equipment to most effectively operate in them, regardless of your species' nature and abilities on land.

Although aerial vehicles allow for travel to any point on the surface of the Earth, they are likely to be very resource-intensive in terms of requiring fuel. Even if the ability to fly is natural to your species, it would still, presumably, be tiring, and there's no point in being able to swoop in to an area if you're then too tired to fight effectively. Most importantly, however, life forms on the surface itself will be able to take shelter and conceal themselves by the simple expedient of ducking under cover.

Buildings constructed in urban areas, ground under forest cover, caves, walkways under overhanging ledges… All of these will provide cover and concealment for native life forms and resources. Sooner or later, therefore, you will have to negotiate ground terrain on Earth, either in person or in vehicles – and most likely both.

Land vehicles of some kind will, therefore, be advisable, even if your physical abilities make them not technically necessary. Whatever your abilities to adapt to the environment, or to move over terrain, it will almost always be useful to have vehicles that can offer protection from attack by human resistance forces or non-sentient animal life, move more quickly than natural mobility allows, and carry heavier weapons and supplies.

Surface Operations

The size of the vehicle is entirely a matter of your preferred doctrine. For example, you may find that you work best operating with individual vehicles, each acting as a protective covering for a single invader, or you may prefer to deploy in transport or assault vehicles that can carry many troops and supplies to a region where you are operating with your natural mobility. This preference may or may not be influenced by the physical size of your species.

Individual vehicles may make more sense if the Earth's gravity or atmospheric pressure is greater than that of your native sphere, or if you lack limbs entirely. Assuming you have limbs for mobility, you may find that powered prostheses will both support your frame against the environment and offer greater speed, strength, and agility than the native humans. This will provide a valuable bonus in any pursuits or melee combat encounters against humans.

If the Earth's biosphere is totally inimical, you are going to need life support systems installed in your vehicles – of any size – and environmental controls to maintain the optimum conditions to support each of your individuals while out and about on Earth. This makes larger vehicles more logical, as more of your forces can crew each vehicle, making a better use of whatever resources are required for you to maintain the environmental systems on board.

There will always be the danger, however, of such a vehicle being damaged or destroyed, or crashing, or malfunctioning in some other way that will lead to the crew and passengers within being exposed to Earth's biosphere. You will therefore still need emergency life-support equipment to support such stranded individuals.

This may be enough of a problem to justify using individual vehicles, which should be as form-fitting as possible on the inside, so that the exterior, whatever its form, is effectively an extension of the occupant. This should be more efficient, especially if the vehicle's external sensors – you will need at least pressure sensors, accelerometers, and temperature sensors – are directly linked to the occupant's nervous system. In this way, the occupant can feel their surroundings as if they were not inside a vehicle, and so will be able to navigate and respond to situations more quickly and efficiently.

The actual means of locomotion will be an important choice for vehicles of any size. Given the wide variety of differing terrains on the Earth's land surfaces, some form of antigravity would be the best option, allowing your forces to move across any type of surface with impunity. Failing this, a form of ground effect cushion – a hovercraft, as vehicles with this feature are called on Earth – is another good choice, allowing free movement over most surfaces, and easy transitions from the land surfaces to water.

The disadvantage to this form of support is that the vehicle must be quite low, and large obstacles will block movement.

Wheels are an obvious choice, and should be as sturdy as possible. The larger the tyres, and the more variable their pressure, the more variety of surface conditions can be traversed. Lowering pressure within larger tyres will allow them to travel over far rougher surfaces, even including fallen trees or plains of stones up to the size of small boulders. Even then, slopes with large boulders or fissures, and forested areas with heavy tree growth, will still be problematic.

Segmented tracks are quite useful for covering many types of terrain, but you must be careful to ensure that the wheels are each given a separate suspension, with as much leeway as possible, especially on the vertical axis. A minimum of three wheels on each side of the vehicle is recommended, even for small single-occupancy vehicles, with the wheels arranged in a triangle. The uppermost wheel should be at least as high as the fore-and-aft wheels are apart, and if the whole arrangement of wheels on each side can also turn and/or rotate as a unit, then so much the better. Such an arrangement should give better steering and navigation ability.

Surface Operations

If the whole triumvirate of wheels can rotate as a single unit, and especially if each wheel is able to be moved closer to or further from the centre on some telescopic mount, you should be able to arrange for a greater climbing ability, both on stairs and exterior natural surfaces.

The most versatile form of locomotion for travelling on Earth's land surfaces, however, is a set of legs. Legs offer far, far more variability in the types of terrain they can cover, and also offer the advantage that it is possible to construct mechanical legs without having to use wheels anywhere. The joints can use spherical sockets, flexible materials, or hydraulics to move.

Ideally there should be at least three legs, and preferably four or more. Despite the bipedal nature of humanity, the bipedal form is actually inherently unstable (bipeds are designed to essentially keep moving forward, rather than even stand still). Although evolution has led bipedal species to use all of their senses in maintaining the optimum posture, it has always proved far more difficult to balance a mechanical device on two legs and make it walk with any degree of speed or stability. If you have the technology to do so, however, then feel free, as the psychological effect of seeing giant-sized humanoid figures wandering around will be effective in giving humans pause. In fact, some societies on Earth are so taken with the idea of piloted mechanical giants that they may even be persuaded to join your side just for the chance to interact with them. Failing that, they may at least be lulled into a false sense of security, and thus lured to an easy defeat while they stop to admire your handiwork.

For a better solution, four legs is more likely to be a workable system, though it would be something of a mistake to have them patterned after humanoid legs, with all four central joints aligned in the same direction. In fact, the optimum arrangement for a four-legged mechanism would have the central joints – the knees – in the opposite positions for the front and rear legs. As with the majority of quadripedal mammals you will find on the Earth, the central joint of the rear legs should be aligned to have their apex at the rear.

Even human cyberneticists have realized this, and begun to construct autonomous transport machines to this pattern, given the name 'Big Dog'.

More legs still are also a viable option; most terrestrial insects have six, and arachnids have eight, and all are particularly manoeuvrable and adept at traversing even the most complex surfaces. Psychological effects on human witnesses and opponents can again be exploited here, as most humans have a revulsion to insectoid or arachnid forms, and utilizing such forms will not only be efficient, but frighten many humans into either not approaching to harm you, or making mistakes in their counterattacks.

You can choose whether to have weapons built in to the vehicles, or simply have the vehicle equipped with manipulator arms capable of utilizing weapons it picks up. The former approach is more reliable, with a solid mounting for whatever weapon, and means you can have the energy supply and/or ammunition supply integral to the vehicle itself. On the other hand, something capable of picking up whatever weapon or tool is necessary at the time – without the need for physical modifications – obviously offers more variety and adaptability. You will need to plan in advance whether you are more concerned with security and reliability, or with the ability to adapt to fluid circumstances.

The type of power source you use – and this applies equally to air and sea vehicles as well as those on land – should be both long-lasting, renewable, and not dependent on being refuelled or recharged in your secure areas or at home. While you will obviously not want the humans to be able to reactivate any vehicles or power units you use, there will be more chance of losing such vehicles to them if they run out of power in human-controlled areas, and can't get back to you.

Surface Operations

It is recommended to use one of the following means of power for your terrestrial vehicles:

1) Some form of miniature fusion reactor, or equivalent. This will be relatively clean, last for years without refuelling or recharging, and can be used as a self-destruct weapon if in danger of being captured.

2) Local fuel sources such as electric motors, diesel or petrol. These are more crude, and you may have destroyed the production facilities in any pre-invasion bombardment, but they have the advantage of not advancing the human technology if they are captured. On the other hand, they can be used against humans if captured, and, on the gripping hand, if you're coming from a parallel Earth this will be familiar technology that will work with your existing vehicles.

3) Bioelectric or psychokinetic power drawn from the occupant(s). This has the advantage of being unstealable, lasting as long as there is an occupant, and not being subject to EMP attack or other energy-draining effects.

The most fundamental and important rule of vehicles for travelling on Earth – especially vehicles designed for a single snug occupant – however, is this: Do *not* rely on small wheels or castors, because there is basically nowhere on the planet, other than some of the better-maintained roads, upon which such a wheel will roll more than a few inches.

ATMOSPHERIC SUPERIORITY

There is a big difference between space superiority and air superiority within the Earth's atmosphere. Space superiority can be maintained with stationary vessels, and the ability to conduct orbital bombardments. Air superiority requires constant movement, either very quickly, with great agility, or in such a way to avoid detection. Air superiority means being able to control traffic in the atmosphere and use that control to exert force upon the surface and upon other atmospheric traffic.

Air superiority is a misleading subject for the tactical planners of an invasion of Earth, or any other planet. In particular, if you have a fleet of starships in orbit it may be tempting to assume that you have air superiority handled. After all, you came who knows how far, you can observe everything that happens in the atmosphere below, and you can target anything moving down there, can't you?

Well, not necessarily. For one thing, it all depends on what weapons technology you brought with you. If you only brought strategic missiles, or mass-drivers, or some form of artillery designed for engagements between capital ships, then you will have a problem. Depending on the ship(s) you have as strategic/tactical support, your weapons systems simply may not be able to hit a manoeuvrable aircraft below, for example. Strategic weaponry simply isn't suited to quick reactions and the flow of an aerial combat.

If you have no backup in orbit, you will also require air superiority for the strategic bombing component of your attack, if you have one. So, you are going to need to dip into the atmosphere in order to establish superiority there.

Strategic bombardment does not just mean dropping rocks from orbit, however effective that may be. Clearly you can assault surface targets with many forms of ordnance, be they bombs, missiles or meteors, and whether they be delivered from orbit, launched from surface installations, or delivered by aircraft. There are many practical reasons for the application of strategic bombardment – to destroy military or manufacturing infrastructure, prevent gathering of insurgent forces, deny areas to enemy forces, and so forth – but one thing it is *not* suitable for is reducing the population's will to resist.

Historically, the military forces of various native terrestrial nation-states have often used strategic bombardment for exactly this purpose, but, historically, it has never worked to that purpose. In every recorded instance, the survivors of the bombed population have in fact simply become more determined to resist.

Therefore, use your strategic weapons as you desire for the practical purposes mentioned above – or indeed simply to eliminate large numbers of the local populace – but if your intent is to reduce their will to resist, then you will be wasting your time using this method.

For both the interception of other aircraft and fast precision attacks on small ground targets, you will need a faster, more manoeuvrable type of craft. Machines suitable for one individual occupant are best, as they can be smaller, faster, and more agile, and carry a decent weapons load.

The weapons load will vary according to whether a craft is optimized for strategic bombing, tactical ground attack, or interception of other aircraft. Currently on Earth, most airborne combats take place at long range, with missiles launched from miles – sometimes even tens of miles – away. The requirement for manoeuvrability in human-built aircraft, therefore, has more to do with the need to avoid inbound missiles than to follow a target around for a close-up attack. Depending on the nature of the weapons you mount on your atmospheric craft, this may not be the case for you.

If you fit your interceptors with light-based energy weapons, the beam should reach the target pretty much instantaneously, considering the distances involved, and so agility will be less of a requirement. If you fit projectile or particle weapons that require visible time to reach the target, or are affected by wind, gravity, or the scattering properties of moisture in the atmosphere, then you will need both speed and agility in order to get closer to your target for a higher probability of a kill.

You will also need greater agility if you intend to either rely on using part of your aeroform as a weapon – for example using a strengthened wing leading-edge as a blade to sever parts of other aircraft – or if you intend to operate at low altitudes where there is a need to avoid buildings, foliage, or geological structures.

Note that human-built aircraft tend to be relatively lightweight and therefore fragile. It does not take a large warhead or a large amount of energy impact to damage one beyond its ability to remain flying. Since your aim should be to eliminate as many enemy craft as possible to attain victory in the skies, there is no need for overkill. Calculate your weapon load to give you the best chance to hit more enemies, rather than fewer chances to do more damage to one. Also bear in mind that, with the object of victory in mind, it is the enemy aircraft you must prioritize, not the pilot (if there is one), so it is not a problem if the pilot survives the destruction of his or her machine.

You may find that you can use the same vehicles as close support craft both in and out of the planetary atmosphere, but this may present difficulties, depending on your systems of motive power and steering.

In the atmosphere, your best mode of steering a fast atmospheric vehicle will be through the use of ailerons and control surfaces built into a lifting body. In other words, you will need a vehicle design capable of being held aloft by the pressure of the air passing under it, and which can be steered by altering the surfaces in such a way as to change how much lift, or in what direction, the airflow gives you.

This is very different from in vacuum, where there is no pressure to steer against, and space-superiority fighters need manoeuvring thrusters and reaction control units for changes of orientation and direction. Your atmospheric craft will require aerofoils and rudders, and will not be able to simply spin around on the spot.

Let's get the disappointing bit out of the way first; saucers are not a good shape for this type of craft, if you are building aircraft locally. Unless you have a solid, stable, antigravity propulsion for saucers, then leave them at home,

Surface Operations

as they will basically be suicide machines in the atmosphere, prone to flipping, tumbling, and crashing. However, if you have stable antigravity and do bring along saucers for atmospheric combat, you will find they give a psychological advantage, at least before your attack becomes widely known, as humans will find it difficult to believe your saucers are actually flying in their airspace, and be reluctant to report an engagement for fear of being considered to be hallucinating.

For high-speed aircraft, you will be better off with a delta shape, with a slim point at the front. The wingspan should be less than the overall nose-to-tail length of the craft, to reduce air resistance. For manoeuvrability of ground attack aircraft, and those operating at lower altitudes as close-support in combat areas, try larger wing areas, with a wingspan wider than the length of the craft. This will give greater stability at slow speeds, and a tighter turning circle.

You will also need a tail with a rudder for steering to one side or the other, and movable flaps on the trailing edges of the wings, for climbing, diving, and tilting to the side.

You can also use rotary-wing aircraft, or what the humans call helicopters. These use a horizontal set of tilted blades spinning at high speed to achieve lift, though most such craft will require a vertically-aligned set of blades at the end of a boom in order to maintain stability and not spin. Most such terrestrial craft have their main rotor set mounted about the fuselage, though there are variations.

If you really love your saucers, it *is* possible to use two contra-rotating sets of rotors at the centre of a saucer-shaped hull, though this will not have great speed or agility. All the same, the most important factor in your aerial adventures in Earth's atmosphere is the ability to shoot down human aircraft without crashing.

Earth's news media is replete with tales of travellers from space who are capable of traversing the infinite gulfs with their magical and near-godlike technology, but who are apparently incapable of noticing where they are in relation to the actual ground. Do not make this mistake. Do not allow the Earth natives to capture and reverse-engineer your vehicles, and to turn their crash sites into tourist attractions. If nothing else, this is embarrassing when you are trying to build a reputation as conquerors feared and respected across the galaxy.

It's even more embarrassing if your pilots are captured, interrogated, or dissected. Note, though, that you do not actually need to have your aerial vehicles carry a pilot. Even on Earth, there is an increasing use of remotely-piloted vehicles and drones, which can be used for reconnaissance and close combat support without endangering an occupant. Since you, as new arrivals, will likely have less access to replacements for lost forces, this is a wise approach to take.

A flying machine can be replaced quite easily, as quickly as the components can be manufactured and assembled, but a pilot's experience cannot be so easily replaced.

SEA POWER

In total, 70% of the Earth's surface is water, and so, while you are living, working, hunting, and fighting on the surface of the planet, you will have to be able to deal with going into areas covered in water. Obviously this will not be a problem for aquatic species, who will only need to concern themselves with the issues of salinity – whether a specific body of water is salt water or freshwater – and the Earth's own aquatic life forms being either food or predators.

If you are a land-adapted species like humanity, or an avian species, you will obviously require, at the very least, adaptation for immersion in water. It's reasonable to assume that if you're capable of having built starships to come to Earth from your homeworld, then you're also capable of

building both aerial and submersible vehicles. If you can make spacesuits to provide you with a breathable atmosphere or protect against low pressures, you can make suits to protect yourselves in water.

Do not, however, be tempted to think that because you have already demonstrated the ability to build a pressurized vehicle for travelling through the near-vacuum of space, that you can simply use the same constructions to travel underwater, no matter how cool SHADO's Skydiver combo from *UFO* or the saucer-shaped flying sub from *Land of the Giants* look when you view those transmissions. Trying to pull off the combination is probably unwise, though not necessarily impossible.

The structure of a mechanical construct built to withstand the absence of pressure is of necessity very different to the structure of something designed to withstand increasing external pressures and the load bearing of immense tonnage of water. At base, a vehicle designed as a submersible will have to be built with a greater attention given to internal supports and bulkheads more evenly spread throughout the design, as opposed to being designed to withstand g-forces at launch, and then zero pressure outside thereafter.

The deepest underwater point on the Earth's surface is 36,200 feet down. That means the pressure there will be 1,097 bar, 1,097 times the pressure of the atmosphere at surface level. The average depth of the Earth's oceans is around 14,000 feet, or 2.65 miles, with a pressure of 424.24 times the atmospheric pressure at sea level. This means any submersible vehicle must be designed and built to protect its interior from that level of external pressures.

Since the mechanical engineering requirements are very different, it would make far more sense to design and use separate vehicles for these environments. It would not be impossible to build one that could be used in the full range of pressures, but the cost-effectiveness in resources would be far less.

You will not need antigravity or the like to power submersible vehicles, or to allow them to ascend and descend. Flooding buoyancy tanks with water will allow descent, and flushing them with air will enable ascent. A submersible or surface boat can easily be powered by any form of storage batteries (so long as they are of the right scale) or power generator, nuclear or otherwise. On the surface, sails are still effective, and used across the globe. This is not a fast or highly technological means of propulsion, but excellent for silent movement and energy efficiency. Under power, a simple screw propeller, or multiples thereof, is still traditional both on surface and submersible vehicles. Propellers cause turbulence in the water, however, called cavitation (it leaves brief cavities, or holes, in the water), and because sound waves propagate even more effectively in the density of water than in air, this makes vessels detectable. A good solution, therefore, is to use some kind of hydrodynamic drive, drawing water in at the front of the engine, putting it under pressure, and squirting it out the rear, as per a jet or rocket engine. As well as being stealthier, this also makes for a smoother ride, and the relative lack of moving parts means there's less chance of catastrophic mechanical failure.

It is also worth considering using the Earth's magnetic field as a power source. It varies geographically and according to the local geology, but is always strong enough that you could use a magnetic drive to move along or across the field. This would be useful if you are using vehicles designed for multiple environments, as it would work equally well on land, sea and in the air. It could be considered a sort of poor man's antigravity, so long as the vehicle remains within the effect of the Earth's magnetic field.

If you're visiting by means of wormhole or dimensional portal, you'll want to make sure that the end destination isn't under water, unless you're from an aquatic species, of course. That said, transitioning to an underwater arrival point would be an effectively camouflaged way of arriving, so long as you are able to ensure that the displacement of the local water does not cause visible surface disturbances, or enough turbulence to affect the passive sonar of ships, or to trigger the various underwater early warning sensors that are positioned on the ocean floor in various areas.

To pull this off, you will have to plan very carefully, well in advance, so that you have worked out how to arrive smoothly. Then again, this is true of any form of arrival at a target you plan to attack, so it should be second nature by this point.

In Earth's history, naval doctrine became vital as human civilization rose, because it was necessary to control the bodies of water in order to carry armies and trade goods. Since the land surface of the planet is so uneven, waterways were much easier options for long-distance journeys. Even now that air traffic is rife, and roads on land have been paved and metalled, and so are able to safely carry massive amounts of traffic and freight, the seas are still a vital part of global travel and trade.

The reason for this is simple; ships can be pretty much any size, and so can transport far more people or cargo than anything else on the planet. This means that you must pay attention to sea traffic and shipping, because it will be used to transport military equipment from areas where you (as yet) have no presence, to areas where the human resistance needs weapons and materiel to use against you.

You'd think that such large ships would be easy to detect from orbit – or even from the air – and destroy, but you might also be surprised. There are 225,625,000 square miles of ocean to search. That will take a lot of processing power to analyse the results your sensors trained on the oceans give you. If you have such good sensors, and enough processing power to spare to analyse their output, good for you – go for it.

Otherwise, it helps to narrow the field somewhat. Thankfully, even on a planet with such a large expanse of open ocean, there are busy areas and bottlenecks, where larger numbers of ships tend to congregate or travel through, and these areas will make excellent killing zones for attacking human shipping.

Some of these areas are busier because they are close to major ports and land-based transport hubs from which arriving cargo can be distributed, or departing cargo can be loaded. Others are busy because they are safe channels that avoid dangers such as underwater reefs or expanses prone to storms.

The best place to attack shipping, therefore, is in the vicinity of ports. The busiest ports in the world are those of Shanghai in China, Kobe in Japan, Hong Kong in China, Dover in England, Rotterdam in Holland, and Los Angeles in the USA. A meteor or nuclear strike on each will largely

Surface Operations

disable humanity's ability to ship materiel by ocean. Doing the same to the Suez and Panama Canals would also be advisable.

The busiest areas of open ocean are the English Channel, the Caribbean, the Arabian Gulf, and the South China Sea, especially around Indonesia. In fact the busiest part of the Caribbean is sometimes called the Bermuda Triangle, and is famed among humans for the number of mysterious disappearances of ships in the area. Most humans seem to be of the opinion that your forces are already at work there, but, in reality, the percentage of shipping passing through the area which vanishes is actually no greater than the percentage of shipping that goes missing globally. It is simply that the area is so busy that there are more ships, so more vanishings.

The existence of these busy shipping lanes is what will make the use of sea power advisable as part of your campaign on Earth. Simply dropping a meteor or nuke on the area will give no guarantee that you will destroy enough ships to prevent them resupplying human resistance. Therefore you will need to blockade these areas, and engage and destroy seagoing vessels as they enter and pass through.

Now, it is true that powered flight will get you and your forces to any point on the globe quickly, and that vessels stationed in orbit can be placed above any point you desire to observe, but a descent from orbit to the surface will still take discernable time, and powered flight, or a starship placed on station-keeping low in the atmosphere, will require a constant fuel supply. The correct shape of hull, however, constructed from the appropriate materials, will simply float wherever you put it on the liquid surface of the planet. You will require ships or submarines.

You can bring your own, build them locally, or even simply commandeer existing ones from their present owners.

Submarines will be the most valuable to you, since these will be able to track and destroy shipping in the blockaded areas quickly, and with less likelihood of detection. Any form of large breach to a ship's hull below the waterline will deal with it quite effectively. If you are used to operating in starships you should be used to the idea of working and fighting entirely within a closed environment that protects you from an inimical exterior, so attack submarines should be quite psychologically comfortable for you.

Capital warships such as battleships will be of little or no use to spaceborne invaders, though their ability to launch missiles and bombard targets many miles inland may be desirable for those who are on a technological level similar to that of Earth in the current time zone. Your own starships should be able to deal with such targets more effectively, and slow-moving surface ships will be easy targets for missiles and air attack. Smaller and faster warships are more useful if you need to board shipping or otherwise conduct operations on the water's surface, though it is recommended that they be protected by orbital or aerial vehicles as cover if possible.

Aircraft carriers may or may not be of interest to you. They are large and relatively slow targets that need protection, but they would also be capable of hosting your atmospheric craft if you wish to have them mobile closer to the surface, rather than based in an orbiting mothership.

Transport shipping is definitely worth considering. Spaceborne invaders do not really need a naval doctrine on the surface, as your projection of power will be from orbit to planetary surface, but other, purely surface-based, invaders will require to be able to move fleets around to transport forces and cargo from conquered areas to unconquered ones. Also, everyone, even spaceborne arrivals, will find that surface ships can store and carry more for less energy expenditure than anything else, which is *always* useful, and enables materiel such as weapons to be stored on the surface ready for quicker deployment. Such ships would also, once air superiority is established, and humanity's submarines and missiles are eliminated, make excellent staging areas on the surface, out of reach of resistance forces.

Considering that huge percentage of the planet's surface that is water, ruling the Earth still means ruling the waves.

WEAPONS AND MARTIAL ARTS

You have safely reached the Earth past its laughably non-existent planetary defences, eliminated major military centres and weapons sites, disabled communications and travel, and landed your forces to engage the current owners – humanity – in your struggle to take possession of the planet for your own nefarious purposes. You have command of the air, the sea, and are swarming all over the land. Well done. The job, however, is not over yet. In the face of a hostile takeover, humanity is not going to just roll over and play dead. If their propaganda, broadcast into the galaxy for the last 80 years or so, is to be believed, they are going to fight back. With tenaciousness and determination in the face of overwhelmingly superior technology, they are going to fight, kick your ass, and then come and invade *you*.

In their dreams, right.

Some of them will come out and fight, some of them will hide and fight, and some of them will talk a good fight, but you are going to keep your nerve, and use the correct weapons and skills for the situation at hand. Your victory will thus be assured.

The term 'martial arts' is normally used on Earth to refer to unarmed combat and, to a lesser degree, to melee combat with simple hand-held weapons with no moving parts, such as swords, knives, spears, and so on. This is something of a misnomer, as any technique for use in combat is a martial art, even one which uses ranged projectile or energy weapons.

One thing that is often forgotten by those who talk a good fight – and those who write propaganda stories, or are involved with the visual arts – is that the choice of not just weapons but even martial arts melee style will vary according to both the mission parameters and the culture from which the warrior originates.

The mission may be geared towards killing your opponents – whether simply as military combat, for sport, for food, etc – or towards suppressing an attack, or even with the intent of subduing specimens unharmed for interrogation, their own safety, or experimentation. You may be from a culture that prizes the ability to kill quickly, or to achieve victory without killing. All these factors will affect both what weapons you use, how you use them, and your melee and unarmed combat. You must bear this fact in mind.

Different objectives and specialist tasks will also require different weapon loadouts and combat skill sets – a demolition mission is very different from a reconnaissance one, and those are different again from assassination or policing actions...

THE RIGHT TOOL FOR THE JOB

Large scale military engagements on the surface of the Earth should be avoided, partly because, if you're doing it right, your control of the air and domination from orbit should make it impossible for the human resistance to actually gather and deploy large units in the field, and partly because such engagements are an unwelcome drain on your resources and ability to rearm and re-supply from your home planet or dimension.

Even among the nations and societies of Earth today, large-scale pitched battles are pretty much a thing of the past, as air superiority and the better use of smaller rapid-response units have taken precedence. Most of your ground-based operations against humans should fall broadly into two categories: ground combat against smaller units of insurgent humans, and policing actions. These types of conflicts will require the use of different types of weapons and tactics, as well as different attitudes. It is vital to make sure your forces are equipped with the right weapons for the task at hand, in the operational environment.

This means, for example, that it is a bad idea to use rocket-propelled grenades when room-clearing in urban areas, as any troops who try that are more likely to blow themselves to bits than to seriously damage the enemy.

If you haven't simply wiped out every human you find, then you will probably also find your forces engaged in policing actions in open spaces, controlling crowds and herding humans. For this sort of action you will require weapons that control and psychologically intimidate, rather than simply kill efficiently. Sonic weapons that cause fear and distress are a good option here, or at least ones that make it impossible for the humans to concentrate and co-ordinate their actions. If these are mounted on impressive vehicles for extra psychological impact, so much the better.

Stun weapons will also be necessary, whether they be electrical, energy weapons, or sonic. This will make capturing humans much easier. If you intend to use the threat of lethal force in such crowd control actions, you should equip your forces with single shot low energy, low penetration wide-area weapons with limited charge or ammunition capacity, equivalent to shotguns on Earth. These will serve the dual purpose of putting down an individual enemy quickly and messily, while intimidating other humans in the vicinity. Such weapons are also less of a threat to your own forces if the crowd should succeed in capturing them.

As an aside, this type of intimidation weapon is also ideal for issuing to any humans whom you enfold into your military as allies or auxiliary forces to boost your on-Earth numbers, as the built-in limitations will prevent them from being the basis of an effective uprising by those who have only pretended to join your side. This is the policy followed by the Goa'uld in arming their Jaffa servants in *Stargate SG-1.*

RANGED WEAPONS

Your choice of ranged weapons will include chemically powered projectile weapons, such as the bullets used by human forces, electromagnetically powered projectile weapons, and energy weapons. All are equally valid choices, and all have their uses and their disadvantages.

Training your forces to use human weapons effectively is a good idea, as it means that ammunition for them can be captured locally, and makes the combat situation less expensive in resources for your side. This will only really work with personal firearms, however, as, although electromagnetically powered weapons – called KEM (kinetic energy missile) weapons or railguns on Earth – do exist, they are to date confined to mountings aboard aircraft and naval vessels. Handheld individual weapons are not yet available.

In open countryside, single shot projectile weapons are appropriate, but be aware that wind and gravity will cause the projectile to drop and veer off course over distances. You can use stronger propellants and heavier projectiles in such areas without fear of overpenetrating targets or the environment and hitting out-of-sight non-combatants or

Weapons And Martial Arts

members of your own forces.

It is as well to use single shot weapons for the simple reason that at greater distances, the target need move less in order for you to miss, so using automatic weapons at long distance will merely result in consuming more ammunition resources. It is better to have an accurate-over-distance single shot weapon and fire when correctly on target. Remember the military truism that the best tactical move is the one that brings you the most gain for the least expenditure in resources.

The same principle applies to the use of energy weapons. The effect of gravity or wind on energy weapons will be so negligible as to be functionally nonexistent over combat distances on Earth, so there's less of an issue with using any kind of rapid fire or burst mode, but single shot will still use less power or charge, while hitting the target instantly (if aimed accurately). Beam weapons that remain 'always-on' while being swept around – such as heat rays, lasers, phasers, etc – are wasteful of energy, since they'll only be doing damage to a target when on target. The rest of the time they'll be wasting energy, and perhaps cutting down trees. Stick to a single effective shot or flash from such weapons; not only will it save energy, but the beam, if in the visible spectrum, is less likely to be traced back to your position.

While it's best to stick to single shot or pulse weapons when out to kill in open countryside, rapid fire automatic weapons and beam weapons will have their uses, particularly in deploying suppressive fire. The machine guns used by human forces, though effective at killing massed troops in a crossfire when set up at either end of a killing ground which those massed troops are entering, are actually even more valuable in dissuading enemy forces from advancing. Essentially, automatic weapons on the battlefield do not necessarily kill more enemies more quickly, but they do enable smaller units to make larger forces stay in shelter. This is, mind you, partly because the use of tight groups of massed troops has fallen out of favour anyway, and such units are unlikely to be encountered. Beam weapons would have the same effect, albeit with the disadvantage of more obviously giving away their positions.

In more confined areas, such as urban centres, inside buildings, and most especially within your own ship or facilities, automatic projectile weapons or energy weapons that fire pulses of energy are more useful, especially with less energy or propellant. Weapons with a burst-fire setting are useful for clearing small groups of enemies constrained within rooms or taking shelter, but it's wiser to use less penetrative ammunition or energy settings. Shots that go through walls have a nasty habit of hitting important items or individuals on the other side.

Quite aside from the risk of hitting non-combatants, it just doesn't do for shots to go through walls and hit power units, fuel stores, or ammunition supplies on the other side, and blow your own forces apart as well as the enemy. If the confined spaces are within your own facilities or aboard your own ships, it's even more important that you do not use weapons that will do damage to vital systems or members of your own forces.

Wide-effect beam weapons or shotgun-like projectile weapons are also effective in clearing enclosed spaces (there's a reason that the pump-action shotgun on Earth is often referred to as a 'trench broom', as it was the ideal weapon for clearing enclosed trenches in which soldiers took shelter.

If you have natural inborn weapons, whether physical – such as claws – or more along the lines of psychokinetic or pyrokinetic ability, then these are best used in the more confined combat areas. In such places, the abilities can be used with greater precision and focus against closer opponents who have less room to escape, whereas in open country there would be far more chance for your targets to flee out of range. Also, of course, such abilities tend to be attuned to closer action in general. Claws, for example, can only be so long.

EXPLOSIVE WEAPONS

You will also need to think about limited area-effect weapons, for use both on open ground, in confined spaces, and against both enemy personnel and vehicles. In other words, grenades, mines, and so on.

As with so many weapons, you can use munitions captured from human forces. After all, their weapons are designed specifically with injuring and killing other humans in mind. This won't even be a matter of choice if you're simply coming from another Earth. Earth-made explosive area-effect weapons come in the form of chemical explosives packed into metal casings and/or with a layer of flechettes, or other metal objects, designed to become harmful projectiles in a spherical area around the weapon upon detonation. If the casing is indeed made of metal, it will be designed to fragment into projectiles itself.

Your technology will hopefully be more advanced than this, and could easily rely upon electrical discharge, nuclear fission or fusion, sonic discharge, and so on. Since it is always best to have as much leeway as possible where re-arming and re-supplying is concerned, it is recommended to use energy-based grenades and mines which can be recharged and reused, rather than ones which are destroyed in the process of being turned into shrapnel or flechettes upon detonation, as those must always be replaced.

If you are using some form of energy-based grenades and mines, whether they be based around light, electricity, radiation, or other forms of immediately dischargeable energy, do try to make sure that they are rechargeable only by equipment belonging to your forces, so that the human resistance cannot recover such weapons and use them against you.

ANTI-VEHICLE WEAPONS

Since there are a wide range of vehicles in use by the natives of Earth, both on land and in the sea and in the air, you must be prepared for the possibility of your forces on foot (or equivalent) encountering them.

You will, of course, have had the sense to use EMP weapons in the early stages of your invasion, but there will always be vehicles that are of old enough technology to have survived in reparable form, or were in shielded bunks, or have been built after the EMP use. You will therefore have a good likelihood of facing individual vehicles in the field.

This is where smaller EMP weapons will come in useful, whether in self-contained grenade form, in mine form, or as directed energy weapons which can be aimed at powered vehicles in order to stop their functioning. Such EMP weapons will not destroy ground vehicles or floating vessels, but will at least render them inoperative, and leave them as defenceless targets for your other weapons. Aircraft, on the other hand, if they are rendered inoperative by an EMP weapon strike, will simply fall out of the sky and be destroyed. Aircraft being faster and able to manoeuvre in three dimensions, however, will be much harder to hit with a directed EMP.

Attacking an armoured vehicle, or trying to bring down enemy aircraft, are circumstances in which beam weapons should definitely be considered. Any form of laser or particle beam that can burn through armour, or slice off a plane's wing as it makes an attack run towards your forces, is worth using. Since Earth aircraft generate a lot of heat, the use of heat-seeking missiles against them is also advisable.

Rockets and missiles are also advisable for use against vehicles when beam weapons are not available.

Of course, no ranged weapon is much use if you don't aim properly, so it's always worth making sure that your weapons have decent sights. Sights using a mix of X-ray, thermal vision, magnetic resonance imaging, and sonar would be ideal, giving you plenty of options to see through walls and identify your targets even when they can't see you.

It would be somewhat unimaginative to rely strictly on the visible spectrum for aiming, since you would be limited by available light and by solid cover between you and your enemies. Even if your weapons cannot shoot through a concealing wall, it is always better to at least be able to see them and track them. A pheromone sensor of some kind is also useful for this, which would enable you to track where enemies had already been, so long as they had been in contact with their surroundings.

Whether you equip the weapons with such sights, or use them in other battlefield equipment such as armour or environment suits, is up to you, so long as the two things can be linked in the perception of the being who is using them.

The most important thing to remember about sights and sensors on your weapons (and on your vehicles, for that matter) is to use *passive* sights rather than active ones. That is to say, sights and sensors that receive incoming light/ pheromones/sound waves/heat etc and turn them into an accurate display for aligning the weapon. Never use sights that project a light or tag on to the enemy, not even a red dot of otherwise harmless laser light, because it's a dead giveaway that you are targeting that enemy, and will allow your position to be identified and counterattacked.

If you absolutely have to project a laser spot onto a target, make sure it's strong enough to be an instant kill in the first place.

FLASH OF THE BLADE

There are as many different kinds of melee weapons as there are people. Spears, knives, swords, maces, flails, you name it. All have their uses, though the variety that are most useful are bladed or edged weapons.

There is little that can be said about blunt trauma weapons. Hit the enemy with a heavy object, it will cause impact damage, rupture cells and tissue, and break bones. Simple, and not really something that becomes any different when upgraded by technology. So long as you make sure a blunt instrument is made of a material which will transfer all its kinetic energy into the target – i.e. it won't bend or break upon impact – and is both solid and fast-moving, you're on to a winner.

Things get more complicated when blades become the subject, as there is a great temptation to move away from using solid materials for the blade, towards using more flexible materials, or even energy. There is a certain sense to this, because there are flexible materials stronger than steel, and energy such as gas plasma, lasers, and electrical arcs can be used to slice and cut.

Powered physical blades with small cutting blades chained together make useful tools for cutting certain types of materials, but actually will not make such effective weapons for your space marines against flesh and armour, because the chains will tend to jam when pieces of bone or body armour etc are caught in the mechanism.

Vibrating blades are almost as useless an idea, and worth avoiding, unless you are carving the meat course at your victory feast – the energy used to vibrate a blade doesn't make it any more effective at cutting, since it's the sharpness of the edge and the mass of the blade that does that.

Many would-be planetary conquerors whose tales are told on Earth seek to use massless blades, or as close to massless

as possible, whether it be in the form of blades made of light, energy, gas plasma, or monomolecular material. A monomolecular filament blade is one made of a single molecule, and so it is invisibly thin.

Monomolecular filaments are a staple of alien knife-wielders, rather than swordsmen. Such a weapon is potentially practical as a short blade such as a knife or dagger, with the single molecule filament able to slide between the more complex molecules of things – other blades, armour, flesh – but they also pose problems for the user. For one thing, a single molecule filament would be so thin that it would be extremely difficult to tell whether the thing was actually there at any given moment. It is also difficult to judge whether such a blade could remain rigid over a full sword's length. Sheathing it would also be difficult, as it would cut through the sheath. In many ways it would be more dangerous to the user than to the enemy.

A blade made of ignited gas plasma would be a practical cutting blade – in fact they're used in manufacturing and construction everywhere – but would not necessarily be able to sustain the full length of a sword's blade. Also, the longer the blade, the more it would vary according to atmospheric conditions and how rapidly it was moved. In the end, such a tool is probably not worth the bother of adapting as a weapon.

When it comes to massless blades, however, one of the most popular concepts on Earth is the lightsaber, a blade made of light and energy, and sometimes described by their owners as 'laser swords'. Laser light is invisible in vacuum or in a still air, which means a lot of users would fall victim to looking down the hilt to see whether it was on, with predictably gruesome results. Not the kind of weapon you will want to issue to forces whose lives will depend on it.

Aside from that, there is the question of just how does one regulate the length of a laser beam to three or four feet anyway? The only way would be to have a physical object at the core of the blade, which a plasma blade wraps around, but this core would be fragile. The lightsaber also has some obvious design flaws even if you can perfect the concept. The danger of accidental activation is obvious.

What's particularly strange about the lightsaber is that its users apparently tend to be those with psychokinetic abilities – that is to say, they can move objects with their minds, their thoughts somehow interacting with the physical world to affect physical objects.

If your species, or at least its military forces, have this ability, then using the physical mobility skills of fencing and martial arts is probably not the best way of engaging in combat anyway. After all, why put your life and limbs at risk when you can simply control the weapon telekinetically, from a safe distance? If your species has psychokinetic abilities, then, depending on how that ability has evolved, you may find that you can in fact weaponize the ability or skill, and use that in place of more conventional melee weapons, at least when in conflict with individual terrestrial natives, or small groups.

Note also that if your species, culture or military forces have extremely strong psychokinetic powers, capable of hurling large objects by the application of mental force directly influencing the physical world, you ought to find that those abilities are far more practical in a combat situation than tiring physical exertion. Why would you want to jump around while trying to wield a massless blade, when you can simply conserve your energy by using psychokinesis to rupture vital organs in your opponent's body or nervous/brain system? At the very least, you should train to use the psychokinetic ability to control the weapon, rather than use physical force unnecessarily, or aim a ranged weapon under physically challenging conditions. Remember that military maxim: the best tactical move being the one that nets you the most gain for the least expenditure of whatever kind of resource – even personal energy. Let the enemy tire themselves out instead.

Of course, other forms of psi abilities would have their own values in combat situations, for example by influencing the perceptions of the human defenders by making them see their comrades as members of your invasion force, or vice-versa. Affecting the perception centres of the human brains may also allow your forces to be edited from the ability of the defenders to see or recognize at all.

Other useful psychic abilities would include the ability to affect the fear centres of the brain so that defenders will simply run away, blind them, destroy their aim, and so forth. In fact the practical applications are almost endless. Such abilities have been referenced in terrestrial literature and entertainments, although, strangely, they have tended to be done so in relation to mutated or enhanced human characters using these skills against or in aid of other humans, rather than in terms of extraterrestrial invaders having evolved such abilities elsewhere, and brought them for use in an operation on Earth.

Of course the reason why solid melee weapons have lasted in use since the dawn of time is because they are always still practical. No moving parts to malfunction, no power source to be jammed by an EMP burst, just simple straightforward practicality. Even in advanced societies with technological defences, the simple blade has its place. Bulletproof body armour can be cut, because the physical effects of the two types of impact are so very different. Energy shielding designed to stop electromagnetic radiation will not react to something as slow and dense as a piece of steel.

The simple knife, bayonet, or sword, therefore, still have their place in melee combat, and the only real reason for not using them would be if your species has inbuilt natural equivalents, such as claws.

There is no need for a particularly large blade – it's not the size that matters, but where you stick it. Humans are relatively fragile, with arteries and blood vessels too close to their outer skins for their own good in combat, and, over the whole human history, the average depth of a fatal piercing or cut is a mere two inches.

Blades do not need to be particularly sharp at the edge, but it helps if they come to a fine point at the end. A curved blade will be more effective if the cutting edge is on the outside of the curve, as there will be more pressure on the target across much less surface area, making penetration easier, and damage greater.

Narrower blades will be more difficult for an enemy to grab and commandeer, with more chance of cutting themselves in the attempt. A wide blade may be more easily trapped and controlled by an enemy. Especially if it has handles built into it all the way along.

A large blade with the blunt edge on the outside of the curve will be fairly effective at deflecting incoming enemy blades if you wield the weapon in such a way as to place the outer curve in the line of attack, but this will, of course, mean that the sharper edge is closer to you, and increase the danger of a push or shove causing it to lacerate yourself or your equipment. If you are the sort of species who prides itself on struggling with extra difficulty as a point of honour, then combining a wide blade with handles all along the blunt outer edge will provide the perfect – if near-suicidal – test of your martial skills, since if you are able to wield it effectively enough to gain victory in combat over humans, you must be a formidable warrior indeed.

The smarter and more efficient and effective warrior, however, will stay away from such weapons as the legendary bat'leth, and use a proper blade instead.

DO YOU KNOW KUNG FU?

If you have come to Earth from a parallel Earth, or from a different era on the planet, your martial arts will still be appropriate and valid. However, if you have come from a different world, with different environmental conditions, you will have to consider altering your styles of melee combat.

We Will Destroy Your Planet

This is the case regardless of how humanoid your species is because of the differences in air pressure, gravity, atmospheric conditions, and so forth. If you evolved on a lower-gravity environment than Earth, for example, you will find your movements slower and clumsier. If you evolved in a different atmospheric composition, you may find that you tire more quickly because the chemicals and nutrients you'd normally acquire through respiration in your own atmosphere are differently balanced – or absent altogether – in the Earth's atmosphere.

What forms of martial arts are best for melee combat against humans? There is no true 'correct' answer to that question – your species obviously has its own preferred means of combat, evolved over however long.

Motive and intent will determine your most useful style of unarmed combat. Obviously the way you fight will vary according to whether you are trying to kill your opponents, subdue them for questioning/slavery/experimentation/amusement, get away from them, etc. The way you conduct yourself in a desperate fight for life will be different than the way you fight to capture a resistance leader with vital information, for example. You will find certain forms of holds and injuries more effective than others against human resistance. The human nervous system is fairly fragile, and vulnerable to pressure and impact damage applied to nerve clusters that are quite shallow under the epidermis. Attacking these nerve clusters can incapacitate or render unconscious. Humans are also vulnerable to damage from the flesh being (easily) punctured. Severing the spinal cord at the third vertebra is fatal, rupturing almost any of the organs by impact or pressure wave is fatal, immersing the head in water for a couple of minutes is fatal, asphyxiation by constricting the respiratory passages for three minutes is fatal… You get the idea.

Humans, of course, also have their many forms of martial arts. You may try to restrict their knowledge of these arts, or their chances to learn them, but this will be a futile effort. Because unarmed combat skills use the same muscles, and some of the same skills, as necessary non-combat arts, it has always been a simple matter for humans to continue practicing martial arts by disguising the moves within other activities, such as agriculture (many weapons were derived from agricultural tools), sport, and even dance (which requires the same degree of balance and spatial awareness).

If your species also combined its martial arts with other activities, or derived the combat skills from other activities, this might aid in deceiving melee opponents, or at least in lulling them into a false sense of security, if they do not recognize what you are doing as a threat to them.

Another issue that you will have to prepare for where unarmed combat skills are concerned, is that any protective military or environmental coverings or equipment your forces need in order to survive in the Earth's climate and environment will interfere with their abilities to use their innate skills. Restrictive equipment will interfere with the ability to move freely, interfering with both speed and agility. You will have to re-train your martial artists in new adaptations of suitable unarmed combat skills, to take these variations and restrictions into account.

There will always be ways around the restrictions, and alternate techniques for any situation, but you absolutely must consider them in advance, as part of your preparations for conducting combat operations on Earth.

WEAPONIZING YOUR TECHNOLOGY

Many forms of peacetime technology and engineering, even on Earth, evolved from weapons and military requirements, simply because, as the saying goes, necessity is the mother of invention. The reverse, however, is also true – you will find

We Will Destroy Your Planet

that many types of technology and engineering lend themselves to surprising military applications, especially in a campaign such as one to conquer the Earth.

Rather than be belatedly forced into adapting technologies for invasion purposes due to lack of planning, or surprises on the battlefield, consider well in advance how you can use all of your equipment to its best effect in the pursuit of victory.

Teleportation, whether by natural ability or technological means, is vastly underrated as a potential weapon, and any invader with the ability to teleport objects by whatever means should most definitely not just be using it to get around, unless the ability is limited to being only able to teleport oneself. In which instance, of course, it is invaluable for penetrating secure areas that could not otherwise be approached.

Even on Earth, where the natives are adept at weaponizing almost anything and everything, matter transmission devices are almost always solely seen as for transporting people and objects. This is distinctly unimaginative; as a weapon, teleportation is an excellent choice for killing or disabling almost anything on Earth. Dematerialize a sphere of matter, say, six inches in diameter, from anywhere on the human body, and that human is out of action. You don't need to rematerialize it anywhere else. Likewise, removing a random volume of matter from any engine will stop it. Do the same to a reactor and it'll probably explode. Dematerialize a section of hull from a ship or submarine, and it will be consigned to the deep forever.

Conversely, teleporting warheads into otherwise protected areas is a good way to take them out, even where a missile or commando strike team would never get through. Don't forget that you can teleport antimatter, if you have any, exactly as easily as you can teleport matter. Generate some in a handy particle accelerator (there are suitable ones in both Switzerland and the USA), teleport it into anything you want disabled or destroyed, and sit back and watch the fun. The possibilities are endless.

Matter-transmission transporters may be the greatest unsung weapons you can use, but there are other pieces of equipment you could do well to adapt. Artificial gravity would be another good choice. If you are able to create and manipulate gravity by technological means, you can make impressively useful mines and anti-vehicle traps by increasing the gravity when triggered, to the point where enemies or vehicles cannot move, or are physically crushed.

If you have the use of force fields or energy shields for protection, don't be afraid to use them offensively as well, as battering rams. As for time travel technology, this can also be used offensively if you can focus upon a target to be moved through time. Rather than simply send targets through to your time, however, you can disable or eliminate them by simply moving *part* of a target through time, ripping the whole apart. Or you can age part of a target to the point where it will decay, at least where the affected and unaffected parts meet. Any starship drive system which warps space can, logically, also be adapted to warp solid matter around it.

Overall, however, make sure that you consider all options in advance, and are prepared with the most efficient and effective skills and weapons for the combat environment in which you will find yourself on Earth.

Do be aware that any human resistance forces who survived the orbital bombardment you should have made will also be doing the same with *their* technology, and will be weaponizing everything they can get their hands on.

This means you will be unable to trust anything you encounter in areas where the resistance operates, and not least because booby-traps will be a primary weapon used by them. Remember that you will now be in a situation of asymmetric warfare, and take appropriate care.

CALLING FOR BACKUP

Being able to refresh, replace, and reinforce your garrison or invasion troops is another vitally important consideration. In fact, one of the biggest obstacles to even the concept of an invasion between worlds is the issue of re-supply and reinforcement over astronomical distances.

If you have starships capable of making faster-than-light or hyperspatial journeys – any sort of trip that will take a matter of terrestrial days or weeks rather than centuries or millennia – then you should certainly instigate a programme of convoys bringing in fresh troops and supplies. Likewise, if you are able to march troops through some kind of temporal or dimensional portal, or teleport them across from your homeworld or dimension, you should be sure to have suitable waves of reinforcements mustered on your side at regular intervals, who can be sent into the campaign.

Otherwise, you are going to be stuck with some rather more difficult propositions when it comes to keeping your forces fresh and in good numbers.

This is where drones, robots, and military AIs in general become worth thinking about. So long as you can use the Earth's metallic resources, you can construct new military AIs and drones on site, rather than having to import them from home. Being able to increase your forces at will is well worth the effort. Just be very sure to protect your manufacturing sites from attack, and to keep the AI programming safe from interference by humans, who will be quick to realise that they can also increase *their* forces by reprogramming yours to attack you.

There is, of course, no reason why any human programmers should be able to interpret a truly alien computer system or language from a truly alien civilization, but the idea of messing up alien invaders by infiltrating virii to their computers has been so prevalent in human propaganda for so long that it is one of the first things the resistance to you will think of, so why take the risk of being complacent about it?

If you have the use of matter transmission technology – and it will have to be a technological process for this to work, not an innate teleportation ability – you may be able to quickly replicate reinforcements, depending on how your system works. Assuming it follows the standard convention of breaking down matter at one end, transmitting the data to the destination, and reassembling the matter there, it would surely be possible – if confusing – to copy the data as it goes through, and re-send it as often as you like. Essentially you could 're-print' as many copies of the same data as you like, allowing you to rematerialize as many copies of the same teleported soldier as you want. This would be a good way to create whole units, or even armies, to spawn directly into the combat area, or at least at your nearest base to the combat area.

This technique could cause psychological problems, of course, with all the copies claiming to be the original, so you will need to assemble a group of volunteers beforehand, who have been thoroughly screened and trained to know what will happen, and understand their situation in advance. It would also be advisable to not send the original volunteers into combat, since they are the original natural ones. How the copies would be treated under your ethical standards – whether they have the same rights as natural-born originals, for example – is a matter for your philosophers, and possibly lawyers.

Otherwise, you have two real options: breeding (including cloning), or recruiting auxiliaries/cannon-fodder locally.

Obviously the problem with breeding natural replacements is that, depending on how quickly your species matures, you could be looking at many years before each generation is ready. Worse still, if they're all individuals with anything resembling free will, they might not want to be part of the campaign when they *have* matured. The same problem applies to true cloning. You can create identical copies of your existing forces at a cellular level, but they still have to be gestated and matured as per normal, and their personalities and minds, having been shaped by a different upbringing than the originals, will not be the same.

You can try to mitigate this by providing the clones with as close to the upbringing and experience of the originals as possible, but there will always be differences. Alternatively, you can try modifying the clones by adding genetic memory and tendencies.

Weapons And Martial Arts

The last option, recruiting auxiliaries locally, is always worth considering. Humans are a violent species, yet also pliable, and can be guided into living certain ways, with the application of authority, religion, or bribery. You may be concerned about the danger of human auxiliaries rebelling, and it's certainly the case that a percentage of them would, but that's why you should give them less effective weapons that will not work against yourselves. A larger percentage, however, would be effectively loyal if treated correctly, because humans are hardwired to belong to tribal groupings. This percentage who are willing to view you as a viable tribal grouping will increase with time. Humans born and raised after your landings will be more used to your presence, and thus more willing to be a part of life with your species.

LIVING ON EARTH

Unless your sole reason for attacking the Earth was to keep your fighting forces in training, to justify their continued existence, or for a simple desire for combat, your time on the planet will not be spent entirely in fighting.

At some point you will have subdued or avoided all local resistance, and be free to do whatever it was that you came to Earth to do in the first place. Perhaps you will be stripping the planet of its resources, to send them back home, or to use in a war effort elsewhere. Maybe you simply need room for your expanding population, or a new home after some misfortune befell your own. Perhaps you even just want a place to visit for fun and recreation. Whatever the reasons, there are things you'll need to think about and be prepared for.

ENVIRONMENTAL AWARENESS, PART 2

Aside from the climate and gravity, which have already been

mentioned, there are many other environmental factors that you will have to take into account when it comes to living on Earth for extended periods of time.

There are many different types of life form on the planet, some of which can prove surprisingly dangerous, whether they be tiny microbes, or large and fearsome predators. Local weather conditions and geological events must be considered when choosing sites for important facilities or landing areas.

If you are intending to stay on the Earth for a long time, for whatever reason, you will have to look at how best to take up residence, and what sort of residence will be best for you. While it is always possible to remain aboard ships in orbit, or even to land them on the surface, there is more practical value in constructing more permanent settlements.

Building cities and settlements is a complex business, as there are so many factors to consider about them, even without military concerns about security and defensibility. You must be sure the geology is stable, the temperature correct, the structure secure against landslides, earthquakes, floods, drought, and so on. The main geological and seismic issues you will face are volcanoes, earthquakes, and tsunami. There are volcanoes and seismic quakes on other planets also, so you are presumably familiar with the concept. The largest volcano in the Solar system isn't even on Earth, actually, but on Mars. Earth, however, has many more volcanoes, some of which have been dormant or extinct for centuries, and others which are still active.

If you come from a hot and sulphurous planet, then you may feel relatively comfortable making a home away from home in one of the Earth's volcanic areas, but otherwise they are generally best avoided when choosing locations for landing sites, planetary defensive emplacements, and large-scale military facilities. There are too many risks associated with areas prone to volcanic or seismic activity, especially near the oceans.

Living On Earth

Many of the Earth's volcanoes are actually to be found underwater. This is because, in general, volcanic and seismic activity is centred along the areas where the planet's tectonic plates – the vast rafts of bedrock that form the main solid crust of the planet, floating on the more viscous lithosphere – meet. Where the edges of the plates meet, molten rock is forced upwards towards the surface, and can emerge through fissures and hollow mountains. Similarly, where these plates meet, and where other fault lines within the plates rub against each other, seismic quakes are triggered. Several of these plates meet in the middle of the Atlantic Ocean, while three of the four sides of the Pacific plate meet other plates under the Pacific Ocean. These underwater tectonic regions have formed underwater ridges of volcanoes.

Where seismic and volcanic activity takes place underwater, there is a danger of a tsunami following the original wave. This occurs when a pressure wave propagates across the ocean at high speed. When it reaches shallower coastal areas, it shortens in wavelength and vastly increases in amplitude. This will cause the water to draw back from the coast first, adding to the amplitude, i.e. the height. A massive wall of water can then hit coastal areas with enough force to smash buildings, carry ships miles inland, and kill thousands.

These areas – coastlines around the edges of the Pacific plate, are best avoided when choosing suitable locations for facilities and landing sites.

Likewise, the central plains of the United States are prone to tornadoes, while the east coast of the US, and the Caribbean islands around it, are prone to hurricanes – massive storms capable of tearing down buildings and completely changing the local geography. You will need to be careful in selecting suitable environments in which to construct settlements and facilities, which are stable and not at risk from either seismic events or extreme weather.

We Will Destroy Your Planet

At the same time, you will want to build in environments that are suitable and comfortable for your species and purpose. This will be easiest if you have come from another Earth, either in the past, future, or a parallel dimension. In any of these cases you should, and no doubt will, take up residence in the same cities or regions on this Earth, as you occupy in your own Earth or time zone.

If you are adapted to a cold climate, your best option is to build in Antarctica, northern Canada or central Siberia. All of these areas are relatively stable, though areas of Canada and Siberia can warm up enough to be home to mosquitoes in the height of summer. If you want cold all year round, Antarctica is the place to go. Of the two polar caps, this southern one is more suited to the construction of cities and spaceports as it is a proper rocky continent, albeit one covered with ice. The northern cap, the Arctic, by contrast, is actually just a floating ice sheet over water, and so is less suited to large-scale building.

The Arctic is also known to be visited by human nuclear-powered submarines from time to time, which are capable of breaking their way upwards through the ice. Obviously this is a vulnerability that you should not accept quietly. The Antarctic is as far as it is possible to get from any of the main military powers on the Earth.

If you need humidity, the most suitable rain forest areas would be those in South America. These areas have the advantage of also being stretched across the southern tropic below the equator, and the tropics are the best latitudes from which to launch vehicles into orbit. If you are adapted to dry heat, any of the North American, African, or Asian desert areas will be perfect. Again, these areas are mostly stable, as is the Spanish desert.

If you are aquatic, the oceans are very welcoming, but bear those ocean floor volcanic ridges in mind. Also bear in mind that the oceans are as filled with life as the land surfaces of the Earth. Although none of the aquatic life forms native to

Earth have limbs of digits capable of manipulating tools, this does not mean that there is no intelligent or sentient life there. Given the prevalence of liquid water on the surface, and its precipitation in the atmosphere, if your species is vulnerable to harm – or dissolution – by water, you should steer well clear of the planet, no matter how suitable its crop fields are as an artistic canvas.

INDIGENOUS LIFE

The range of species currently occupying the Earth is incredibly diverse, although merely the latest in a long line of life forms over the planet's four and a half billion-year history. The main types of life you will encounter there are: plants, fungi, bacteria, virii, insects, molluscs, fish, reptiles and amphibians, birds, mammals and exotic undersea creatures. All terrestrial life forms are made up of organic cells, constructed of a nucleus surrounded by protoplasm. The number of cells varies between life forms from one only, all the way up to hundreds of trillions.

PLANTS, LICHENS, AND FUNGI

Non-mobile life forms that absorb liquid and nutrients via the soil, and use sunlight to convert carbon dioxide into oxygen – plants – are eaten by most forms of life on the planet, and also depend on other life forms – often insects – as a vector for carrying spores and thus enabling reproduction. Very few plants consume animal or insect life directly, but there are a few that deliberately entrap insects or small mammals.

Plant material is used as a food source by pretty much all life on the planet – even carnivorous predators also consume plant material for certain nutrients, or to assist with digestion.

Lichens and fungi are similar immobile species, though they have a different cellular construction, and do not have the male and female genders, which true plants do.

Other plant material, called wood, especially from the larger types called trees, is also useful in construction and manufacturing, and you will probably find wood useful in many ways. It is also recycled into paper, upon which documents and even books about conquering the Earth are printed. This, if nothing else, proves that plant material is of vital importance.

Some plant material is nutritious while others are poisonous. Since you will need to arrange a food supply during your stay on Earth, and importing everything is both a resource expense and a potential vulnerability to attacks that could weaken your forces (and therefore your hold on the planet), you should be sure to test all organic materials for suitability for conversion into food. Even material which is either ineffective or actually harmful in its raw form can be processed into something useful, with the application of correct research and treatment.

INSECTS

Insects are the most common visible form of life on the planet. Single celled bacteria may be more numerous, but they are not visible to the naked (human) eye. Insects generally are, and there are also more insect species than any other type of life on the planet.

Some fly, some crawl, some are terrifying to humans, while others are merely repulsive. The insects are, however, essentially the unseen below-stairs staff of the Earth's biosphere, performing vital tasks in both recycling dead and decaying materials, and ensuring the spread of plant life by pollination.

FISH AND OTHER SEA CREATURES

Fish are aquatic animals adapted to filtering oxygen from water by means of gills that allow oxygen molecules to be absorbed into the bloodstream by osmosis. There are many species of many sizes, not with manipulative limbs. Most species are used as a food source, particularly by humanity.

There are predator species of fish in various sizes, from small piranhas to the huge great white sharks, which are capable of consuming humans and even of damaging water-borne vehicles. These creatures should be avoided.

The oceans are also home to cephalopods, tentacled creatures with multiple brains and hearts, quite unlike anything else on the planet. Some of these cephalopods are large enough and powerful enough to – according to local legend, anyway – attack and sink surface vessels such as boats and shipping. In fact the most alien creatures, compared to the standards of the human population, live in Earth's waters, including strange single-celled creatures that congregate around lava vents in the deepest high-pressure areas, and life forms which are neither truly animal nor vegetable, but somewhere in between. Perhaps even with a bit of mineral thrown in to complete the traditional set of organic elements.

BIRDS

Birds are the Earth's avian species, and in fact are direct descendants of the prior dominant species of the planet, the dinosaurs.

There are both flighted and flightless species of birds, and even a few aquatic species which 'fly' only underwater. This latter tendency should not be a surprise, as it is still movement in a full three dimensions, which relies on planed limbs for manoeuvring.

Birds should be no threat to an invading culture. As well as being a potential food source themselves, birds also are an egg-laying life form, rather than giving live birth, and the infertile eggs are a common food source on Earth.

REPTILES AND AMPHIBIANS

Unlike the other animals on the planet, reptiles are cold-blooded, with a much lower body temperature and no internal means of regulating that temperature. They too are egg-laying creatures.

Some of the reptile species – in particular the crocodilians – have been around since the time of the dinosaurs, which had led most humans to believe that the dinosaurs were themselves reptilian. However, it has subsequently been discovered that those dinosaur species that were not made extinct at the K/T impact later evolved into birds. This suggests that the other dinosaurs were, like birds, warm-blooded, and thus not reptiles. That would mean that the reptiles were always cold-blooded.

Since reptiles have been around on Earth for hundreds of millions of years in a relatively unchanged form, some believe this is a sign that aliens such as those of you now invading the Earth could quite likely be reptilian in form, if the pattern of reptile evolution is a universal norm, and there was no K/T impact on a reptile planet.

Of course, if your species is itself a form of reptilian or dinosaur life having travelled forward in time from before the K/T impact, you will already know about these species. Many humans consider reptiles to be frightening or unsettling, and this may be worth taking advantage of.

MAMMALS

There are only 5000 mammalian species, but they are the ones that you will be most concerned with while living on Earth. The most notable mammal species is, of course, the dominant humanity, but there are many other species sharing the planet with them.

Mammals come in many different sizes, and vary between two and four-legged species. Some have been specifically husbanded by humanity as food sources – cows and pigs, for example – while others such as sheep are bred for their outer coating. There are many large predator species of mammal, but also small scavengers and rodents. Not all mammal species live on land: dolphins, seals and whales are mammals despite being aquatic.

Although the human species considers itself the dominant intelligent species on the planet, it is neither the only intelligent species nor the only one that could pose a threat to your plans for the world. Taking these issues in order, the first thing you must bear in mind is the existence of other species who may be at least as intelligent, but who simply have not evolved the physical capability to mechanically affect their environment.

On land, the apes are the closest species, genetically, to humanity, and so they naturally are close in intelligence also. There are some gorillas which have been taught to communicate with humans, and also various of the ape species are adept at using tools, and have complex social interactions, as do humans. The elephant, the largest land mammal, is also very intelligent, and has been known to display both mathematical skills and artistic talents.

In the oceans, the dolphin species is thought by local scientists to be as intelligent as humans, if not more so. They are famous for displaying empathy with not just others of their own species, but with other species that venture into the water as well. While these aquatic species are intelligent, they are unlikely to pose much of a threat to you. Even if they become hostile, they do not have the means to use weapons.

The type of threat that you will face from various other life forms on Earth is going to be in the form of attacks from predator species, and also from defensive strikes from venomous reptile and insect species.

Predator attacks are going to be the most effective, and the ones that you must guard against. The claws and fangs of the various large predators on Earth will be equally effective against any form of organic tissue, regardless of its planet of origin.

If your species is small in size – say less than one or two feet in height or length – you may find that insect and reptile species attempt to prey upon you, with the use of chemical venoms meant to paralyse or kill. If you are larger, you may still trigger defensive or territorial attacks from these kinds of creatures, even if they are not motivated by viewing you as prey.

Whether the venom from such creatures will affect you, or do so in the same way as it would affect native terrestrial creatures, is impossible to determine without study. You should certainly obtain samples for testing, and to produce antivenom if necessary.

BACTERIA AND VIRII

Disease, germs, virii and bacteria are actually much more likely to be a problem if you have come from a parallel world or different time zone on the Earth itself, than if you have from a different planet elsewhere in the galaxy.

The reasons for this are due to the way that such biological agents evolve, and the way in which resistance to them works. Specifically, while some exposure to bacteria and virii can trigger the immune system to recognize them and build resistance to that strain, so the absence of exposure over generations will result in that immunity or resistance being

lost, as the human DNA mutates. Also, the viral life forms themselves will also mutate in attempts to out-evolve both resistance and drug treatments.

The practical upshot of this is that if you come back in time from a future Earth, you will find that biological threats in the target era are adapted to affect humans of that era, but any such bio-agents which have been eliminated between the target era and your own will be *more* dangerous. With those bio-agents no longer a threat in your era, you will almost certainly have lost your resistance to them, which local humans will have due to exposure. The bio-agents, however, will more likely still be perfectly adapted to you, being human, and thus their effect will be more devastating upon your forces than upon the more resistant humans native to the target era.

Conversely, new diseases and bacteria will have evolved in your era, which are capable of affecting the people of the target era. You must be careful not to carry these back in time to the target era, as not only will they be effective against a population which has no resistance to them yet, but you will risk causing a paradox in which a pathogen from your era wipes out your own ancestors.

There is a similar danger of cross-contamination for those invaders coming from parallel worlds, though at least in their case there is no need to worry about the potential for temporal paradox.

Those of you coming to Earth from other planets will doubtless also bring assorted bacteria with you. It is believed that bacteria are capable of surviving in dormant form in space, living on asteroids and surviving meteoric impact with the Earth's surface. In fact, the theory of panspermia suggests that microbial life is capable of originating from base chemical compounds and amino acids almost anywhere, and that comet and meteor impacts may have brought it – or at least some forms of microbial life – to Earth in both the past and the present.

This means there is already good reason to believe that alien bacteria could thrive on Earth, building its way up into life from the simplest chemical compounds. But what about the other way round?

Most people on Earth believe that the Martian invaders of whom H. G. Wells did such a good job of reporting in *War of the Worlds* were wiped out by native virii – specifically the common cold (a viral infection affecting the respiratory system and eyes). The popular belief is that the Martians are killed by their lack of immunity to this virus, and that therefore germ warfare would be a practical option for defending against future invasions. However, this is not actually the case.

Examining the original text shows that what attacks the Martians are in fact necrotic bacteria – the bacteria that decompose the flesh of deceased organisms. This occurs because the Martians are not recognized by terrestrial bacteria as alive, and therefore are treated as dead, and disassembled on a cellular level. They are in fact decomposed to death.

Thankfully, this is actually an unlikely event to happen to you, though it does happen even to humans, in the form of necrotizing fasciitis.

The good news is that you will probably not – if you come through space from a different planet – have to worry too much about virii, because they have spent millions of years evolving and adapting to affect terrestrial species. This is, after all, how they best survive. In fact, humanity – and the other species living on Earth – would have more to worry about from the bacteria you bring, as those bacteria are more likely to be robust basic bacteria, ready to adapt themselves to new environments and life forms, as happens in the previously-mentioned panspermia theory.

FOOD, GLORIOUS FOOD

When it comes to food, it is said that there cannot be a creature on the planet that the humans do not cook and eat. If any of the foodstuffs on the planet are suitable for you, then that is an excellent advantage. If you are trying to pass as human, though, take care not to be seen eating anything that the local culture considers repulsive – such as live rodents – as this will arouse suspicion.

We Will Destroy Your Planet

Discovering a food source on Earth is a task not to be undertaken lightly. It will be of vital importance, and it will also bring with it certain implications that are not at first obvious.

It is utterly vital that you test every type of organism on the planet – from the smallest bacterium to the largest cetacean – with which you are likely to come into contact. You will need to know whether any of them are pathogenic to you, and you will need to know which, if any, of them are capable of providing your species with nourishment. You will also need to know if any organism is likely to have an unexpected non-fatal effect on your forces, such as causing allergic reactions, dizziness, sensory interference, neurochemical imbalances, drunkenness, or whatever.

If your tests identify any organic material as being digestible by your species, and that your bodies will absorb nutrients from, this is not all good news. On the one hand, it does mean you do not need to import all your food supplies from home, but the cloud to that silver lining is that it means bacteria which can affect those organisms can be absorbed by you, and could kill you.

ALLIANCES AND ASSISTANCE

There is no reason not to use other life forms – native terrestrial ones or extraterrestrial – as helpers, or even as weapons. The concept is older even than sentient life on Earth, as mutually co-operative arrangements have lasted a long time. Obviously humans have domesticated many creatures, such as horses for transport, dogs as guards, etc, but other creatures across the planet have done it too. For example there are birds that certain large predators such as crocodilians allow to clean their teeth for them; there are remoras, which protect sharks from parasites; and many other such relationships.

Living On Earth

You may find, therefore, that it is useful to either recruit certain humans to perform menial duties, or, if humans are simply too rebellious and unreliable, you can always train other creatures for certain duties. Aggressive predators, for example, can be trained to patrol important exclusion zones and attack intruders. Other territorial animals can be conditioned likewise, or equipped with cameras and sensors to increase security without requiring the use of more of your forces.

Longer-term but forgettable assistance from other life forms can come in the form of plants, or similar in-place life forms. Anything that has thorns or poison harmful to humans can be used as a living barrier, to help keep humans out of important areas.

In the eastern hemisphere, the preference is for alien invaders to make use of the availability of large saurian and other life forms, possibly survivors from the dinosaur era or mutations created by unwise use of nuclear power, and to use them as weapons.

Unlike the early 20th century practice of using flocks of sheep to clear paths through minefields and other booby-trapped areas, the use of these so-called kaiju is more like unleashing a weapon – the kaiju in question can be used to destroy large areas of cities, either by controlling their brains remotely, or simply relying on their tendency to do so when on land anyway. If you can find examples of such beasts, they are most useful for distracting human military forces, prior to your main attack.

Given the interstellar distances involved, and therefore the time and expenditure of resources necessary to transport troops and officials, it actually makes more sense under certain circumstances for you to set up a client state on Earth, than to rule it by force of numbers.

Under the client state model, you would offer the local populace self-determination and the freedom to carry on as they have done, subject to your approval of leaders and of policies that would affect your objectives. For example, you would appoint a planetary governor from your forces, with suitable enforcement units and military backup, who would oversee that the correct local leaders were chosen, and that the resources you require are shipped back home. This approach has worked for thousands of years on Earth.

Alternatively, you can consider making alliances with existing Earth authorities. This is an especially useful approach if you have a preference for hands-off rule, have difficulty understanding humanity and life on Earth, or do not have the military power available to be projected effectively on Earth. Since you will doubtless have technology, if nothing else, that is desired by humans, you can forge an alliance for mutual benefit, or at least the appearance of such, by exchanging a few such technological trinkets for the kind of co-operation you require.

Such alliances can be genuine, or you can use them as delaying tactics while you conduct reconnaissance of the planet and study its defences or move your forces into position. You can use an alliance with humans to lull them into a false sense of security by pretending to be friendly visitors, and thus sow the groundwork for confusion that will inhibit the effectiveness of resistance later. For example, you can do this by offering medical advances, or enfolding certain preferred groups within your alliance while shunning others; divide and conquer is classic strategy for a reason.

NOW THAT YOU HAVE IT, WHAT WILL YOU DO WITH IT?

Why *did* you come to Earth? Nobody embarks on a distant military campaign for no reason at all. Just because you have conquered the Earth doesn't mean your work is over. Quite the opposite, in fact.

MINING THE EARTH'S RESOURCES

If you came to mine the Earth's resources, you will need to be able to make use of them once you have mined them. At the very least you will need to be able to ship those resources back to your homeworld, or to wherever they are going to be put to use.

If you came by wormhole, dimensional portal, matter transmission, or time portal, you shouldn't have any difficulty in transporting you booty back home. Just as the planet's current owners transport their resources by ship and ground vehicle, you should be able to do the same, and simply pass containers on through the wormhole, or beam them to wherever they need to go.

Sending the materials to a different planet through space is a different matter. You can bring in ships to carry it off, but the more material you try to launch, the more fuel your ships will require, which makes them heavier still, and every load is another chance for something to go wrong with a valuable ship. Therefore you would be better off using a mass driver capable of accelerating cargo to the Earth's escape velocity. Rather than repeat the mistake of the Centauri, who wasted such devices on bombarding a planet, you would use it for its intended purpose, launching compacted raw materials of whatever kind into space.

You wouldn't be able to shoot the materials all the way home, because the payloads wouldn't be able to be accelerated to faster-than-light velocities – and even if you did, that'd just mean you'd essentially fired a giant gun at your home – but you could certainly put shipments of cargo easily into orbit. There, your transport ships can scoop them up and take them to whichever planet they need to go to, or indeed just process the materials in the microgravity of space and make whatever products from them that are required, without any deformations caused by a planetary gravity.

The same principle applies to anything you want to launch from Earth – foodstuffs, plant material, anything.

The best place to construct such a mass driver would be on the western slope of Mount Chimborazo in Ecuador, at the north end of the Andes mountain range. This is not the highest mountain on Earth – that would be Everest in the Himalayas, of course – but because the planet bulges slightly in the middle, Chimborazo is about a mile and a half closer to orbit. The western slope should be chosen because the Earth spins west-to-east, and so launching towards the east always imparts an extra flick of velocity.

Of course, major mining operations will require more than one mass driver, but this should set the pattern: building them on the western slopes of mountains in the equatorial band bordered above and below by the tropics.

Oddly enough, this is one of those situations in which completely destroying the Earth is actually feasible. It just would take a very long time. In fact, removing a million tons from the Earth every *second* would completely remove the Earth from existence in 186,015,123 years, if the effect of having a large percentage of its mass didn't result in the force of its rotation tearing the rest apart in half that time. Interestingly, humanity itself already has the technology to do this if they really wanted to, so it would be a far simpler matter for a more advanced invader.

REPLACING THE EARTH'S CORE WITH AN ENGINE

Removing the Earth's core while retaining the rest of the planet's surface, as seen attempted twice by the Daleks, is, sadly, not physically possible. This means that it won't be possible for you to remove the core and replace it with a power unit in order to drive the planet around, no matter how attractive the idea is.

One issue with it would be how big an engine you would need to pilot the Earth, and what type of engine – where would the exhaust for the thrust emerge, and what would it do to the atmosphere in the process. Not to mention the fact that the core of the Earth is nearly three thousand miles across, which is a lot of space to be filled.

The bigger problem with any attempt to eject 'the molten core of the Earth' through any sort of mineshaft or excavation is that the actual inner core, at the very centre of the planet, isn't molten. Instead it is a ball of solid nickel-iron some 1,560 miles across. The molten core is a layer 1,400 miles thick wrapped around that. Even if you could draw out this magma, you'd still be left with the solid inner core rattling around inside.

There's really no excuse for the Daleks to have not known this, as the solid core was originally discovered by humanity in 1936, when seismologist Inge Lehmann calculated it from the propagation of seismic waves recorded during earthquakes. That said, study of the temperatures of the Earth has shown that the inner core has been cooling to its current temperature of 5430C since the planet formed four and a half billion years ago. At some point in the past the entire core of the Earth has been molten, but as it has cooled from the inside out, the solid inner core has been growing.

This may show the value of remembering that if you are studying the Earth from a great distance away, the conditions there will have changed by the time you arrive.

YOUR PLANET, YOUR RULES

There are many ways of ruling a conquered territory, whether directly, by taking up residence and being in charge on a permanent basis, or more remotely, by issuing orders from a central throneworld and leaving it up to individual planetary governors to decide how to get the best out of their charge. As with so many other things, how you rule the Earth will depend on your motives for conquering it, your numbers in the vicinity, and your attitudes to your own culture and society in comparison to others.

Regardless of these factors, some things are going to be necessary no matter what. One is that you must establish that you are in charge. You do not have to rule by fear and terror, but even if you are magnanimous in victory and magnificent in your benevolence and granting of freedoms, you must ensure that the population understands that it is your decision to make it so.

If you choose to rule the Earth by fear, holding it in an iron fist (or claw, or tentacle, etc), you must be sure that the population fear and respect you. If you threaten violence for transgressions, you must follow through on that threat, or you will be perceived as weak. Your decisions must be understood to be decisions, not suggestions or requests. The disadvantage to ruling by fear is that it will tend to provoke resentment, and that will lead to resistance and rebellion.

Conversely, if you allow the Earth to carry on as it did before, with a self-determining population, you may run the risk of that populace returning to conflict among themselves, which will get in the way of your plans.

The golden rule for ruling however is this: don't flip-flop. If you want to rule by fear, rule by fear. If you want to rule benevolently, rule benevolently. However else you wish to rule, rule that way, but most of all be consistent. Consistency will carry you further than wisdom or military power on Earth, simply because human societies prefer the maintenance of a status quo.

One important information resource with which you must familiarize yourself, of course, is the legendary 'Evil Overlord

List', which contains many practical tips for being the evil (or otherwise) overlord of a planet.

COLONIZING

Did you come to expand your empire or replace your homeworld? If so, then bringing your own population to the Earth is a necessity. Whether or not to do something about the native population is up to you. If there are very many of you, or you have slightly different environmental or climate requirements which will necessitate changes to the Earth, then you will have to look at eliminating or moving humanity.

If you are happy to share the planet, then you will probably have to make sure that the local population know who's in charge, and accepts that the superior newcomers have the edge. Note that even if you have no intention of declaring superiority, or have laws about not interfering with the natural development of native species, this will occur anyway. Historically, no contact between a technologically superior society and a technologically inferior one has resulted in anything other than the inferior society being absorbed into the superior one, and changed by it.

Depending on how rough the conditions on Earth are, there is a chance that your own forces or population might feel disinclined to remain there, especially if there is an easy way to return home. You may consider disabling your own ships to ensure that your colonists have to remain and make the colony work. Make no mistake; however superior your technology, setting up a viable colony on Earth will be hard work, requiring the building of suitable cities, systems put in place to ensure that edible food is available for your species, and so on.

'Terraforming' may be necessary in order to make the Earth completely suitable for your population, but please note that if you came to radically change the place, you'd have been better off consulting the chapter on destroying all humans, since keeping them around will cause you endless trouble later.

Strictly speaking, you can't actually 'terraform' the Earth, since the word means to make something like the Earth. Which the Earth, of course, already is. You can still alter the planet's environment and geology, but the phrase for doing this to the Earth itself is 'Geoengineering', or you could call it planetary environmental engineering. Of course your forces will be more likely to refer to the process as 'forming'.

The concept is known on Earth, having been originated by the astronomer Carl Sagan, in 1961, though he originally called the process 'planetary engineering'. His original suggestion was that Venus be seeded with blue algae, to facilitate the conversion of water, carbon dioxide and nitrogen into organic compounds. (Do not be tempted to try this on your way to Earth – Sagan had the idea before it was discovered that the clouds of Venus are mostly composed of sulphuric acid, which would destroy such algae. In 1973 he revised his suggestion to engineer Mars instead, and the space agency NASA held a study on this, though they called it 'planetary ecosynthesis'.)

The word 'terraforming' itself was coined in 1982 by Christopher McKay of the British Interplanetary Society, in a paper discussing, again, Mars.

Note that if your requirements for a planetary colony require a mostly carbon dioxide atmosphere, with either acid rain and much greater surface temperatures than on Earth, or a thinner and colder atmosphere, you would be better off simply colonizing Venus or Mars, respectively. Those planets would be more suited to your needs for less resource expenditure, and have the advantage of not being occupied by a species who will resist you. As far as anyone knows, anyway.

Likewise, if you are going to terraform the Earth, you should have wiped out the surface life with an asteroid bombardment first. If you're making major changes to the biosphere, the native life will be killed in the process anyway, and this way you can start with a clean slate, without having to worry about sabotage or interference.

PERHAPS CONQUEST ISN'T NECESSARY

Believe it or not, there are several contexts in which it is possible to take up a necessary or desired position on Earth without having to expend the time, effort, or energy in conquering it.

In most of these cases, making alliances with native factions will be perfectly serviceable, and you can always betray them by launching a proper attack later if you so desire. In some other cases, conquest would simply be non-applicable, or even counter-productive.

As well as making alliances, it may be less resource-intensive to trade with the native humans for what you want, or even to actually make friends with them.

GARRISONING

Establishing a military garrison on the planet may be necessary, if you're looking to prevent activity by other civilizations in the vicinity. It may not, however, be necessary to conquer the Earth in order to establish a garrison there. In fact, it may not even be desirable to do so. This is one of those situations in which simply making peaceful overtures to terrestrial authorities may well achieve the result you want: permission to establish a garrison.

This is because, since humans are already quite preconditioned to accept the idea of hostile forces among the stars, it should be a relatively simple matter to establish that your enemies are bent on the conquest of the Earth. With careful manipulation of the collective psyche it should even be possible to persuade human forces to form the bulk of your

garrison, risking their lives under your guidance so that your forces don't have to. Aside from negating the need to conquer the Earth, this also has the advantage of sparing your forces for more important duties elsewhere.

SEEKING SANCTUARY

It's always possible that you came to Earth in order to escape some persecution, warfare, or other threat elsewhere. In this instance, you may find it more useful to simply ask the local populace for help, or at least to manipulate them into getting what you want, rather than causing yourself more trouble. This is especially the case if you have no means of returning home or moving on, or if your equipment is limited by your situation. Also, if you're looking to hide, then conquest is very conspicuous, and so likely counterproductive.

Think instead about setting up an Alien Nation in the US, or living in District 9 in South Africa...

On second thought, don't do either of those things. You didn't come to Earth to be viewed as inferior either. Your best course of action if you are seeking sanctuary or political asylum on Earth is to work with some appropriate shadowy government cabal or agency – or better still, several, in different nations, so that you can spread your population over a wider area, and move on as and when one agency betrays you – who will make sure you are covertly re-homed on Earth, usually in return for technology or scientific and mathematical formulae.

Be warned, though, that some such agencies have been reported as willing to abduct and conduct medical experiments on aliens, rather than waiting for you to do it to them.

UPLIFT HUMANITY

Those of you who have parental interest in Earth may decide to make yourselves known in order to avert disaster or improve humanity's attitudes and morals. In many ways this is just as arrogant as the invaders who feel themselves superior to non-spacefaring civilizations, as it implies that you have a right to judge other species, and determine their worth.

Deciding that unworthy species should be improved and uplifted rather than destroyed is certainly a more reassuring option, but it still smacks of what humans call the 'nanny state'.

Though arrogant, this can be achieved by negotiation as well as direct conquest. The benevolent nanny state society can still invade and conquer the Earth for its own good, but you will find that humanity is more receptive to your teachings if you instead offer rewards for learning the right lessons. This approach also works for slavers and military recruiters, of course.

You do not need to be entirely selfless to take this approach, of course. You could well be concerned about turning humanity away from an aggressive expansionist path before it gets too much of a foothold in space.

Another far more practical reason for uplifting humanity is if you have become stranded, and require a superior level of technology to be attained in order for you to repair your ship or otherwise complete preparations for your return home.

NATURAL INSTINCT

It is possible that you are a non-sentient creature of some kind, and that your arrival on Earth was by pure chance, perhaps carried by an unsuspecting sentient traveller. If this is the case, your whole objective in life will be to survive and possibly reproduce.

Since if you're not sentient you won't be reading this, there is very little advice that can be given, other than to watch out for hunters, either human or otherwise. Certainly you will have no need to conquer the Earth in order to roam wildly, and nor would you ever conceive of doing so anyway.

For what it's worth, general advice for such a species would be to make sure to find a suitable location in which to create a nest or den, because hunting is a popular pastime in most regions of Earth.

THE MOST DANGEROUS GAME

On Earth, the human race often refers to itself as the most dangerous game, in the context of big game hunting, or hunting animals for sport. If such hunting is a part of your society's life, then it may be worth considering using the Earth for this purpose.

The wide range of terrain and environments make for a good choice of types of chase. Although human bodies are relatively flimsy, you may always find, or even breed and train, specimens who will give the most satisfying chase, or prove to be worthy opponents in physical combat to test their mettle.

If you are going to engage in blood sports on Earth, you will not necessarily need to conquer the planet in order to do so. There are enough remote areas of all kinds for you to conduct hunts without being disturbed by human authorities in most cases, though you will have to ensure that your prey do not bring others into the game. You may even be able to gain permission for such hunts with the collusion of terrestrial governments, who may be willing to give you their enemies or criminals for the purpose.

THE PLANET OF FUN

You also will not need to conquer the Earth if you simply want to blow off some steam by having some raucous fun, blowing stuff up, recreational fighting (Glasgow has been good for this sort of weekend off for aliens since Victorian times), and so on.

So long as the native authorities and militaries do not have the ability to seriously harm your holidaymakers and their activities, it doesn't matter whether they know about you or not. You can simply carry on enjoying yourself in whatever way takes your fancy.

There is so much to see and do on Earth that you could simply enjoy yourself for years, with every whim catered for, and nothing to stop you. Visiting the Earth simply to see the sights, insult the natives, play pranks on them by strutting up and down making 'beep beep' noises, or destroy things that don't matter to you for the sheer joy of it, are all perfectly valid reasons for going.

Why shouldn't the Earth be a vacation spot? It has many beautiful sights. If you want to sample the sights, the food, the sports, or just to have whatever your society considers to be a good time, there really is no need to mount an expensive and complex military campaign.

GOING NATIVE

Well, it does happen from time to time that visitors to the planet are either so taken with the lifestyle of humanity that they decide to join in, or are stuck for so long that they assimilate into a human lifestyle by exposure over time becoming habit-forming.

This is far more likely to happen to visitors who have crashed, been exiled, or otherwise ended up living on Earth

Living On Earth

for extended periods not by choice. This, logically, will happen to individuals rather than societies. And so conquering the Earth would be neither practical nor desirable. By doing so, the adopted native will be denying their preferred status.

If you find yourself in this situation, probably by trying to blend in at first, you can try seeking help from government agents with suburban families or interested amateurs.

CARE AND
FEEDING OF
YOUR HUMANS

If your interest in the Earth is in its strategic position or mineral/chemical resources, you're probably wondering what would be the point of preserving some humans. After all, they're going to get in the way, resist your control of the Earth, try to prevent you from actually getting at all those resources you want, and generally prove themselves to be a nuisance.

There are several reasons why you, as triumphant planetary conquerors, may decide to try to keep humanity around, some more obvious than others, and some more practical than others.

Enslavement. Humans are apparently often considered excellent work machines. Nothing can crawl into a narrow crevice in a quarry and carry out some rocks to dump on the rock-crusher's conveyor belt like a human can. According to most theorized alien invasion reports and propaganda stories, there is usually little regard for the health and well-being of these organic work machines. This is, of course, highly inefficient and generally motivated by an immature desire to play at being powerful; in reality, healthy and happy workers are always more productive.

You will undoubtedly find that offering the carrot rather than the stick is generally more effective in motivating your workers. In fact, rather than openly enslave them, and thus generate resentment and rebellion, you should simply offer the population jobs in which they will be paid in the local currency. Since Earth's currencies will mean nothing to you, this will increase productivity while decreasing the odds of resistance and rebellion.

Food. The Earth is teeming with life, pretty much all of which depends, in some way, upon consuming the biomass of other life forms. Since humanity is the dominant life form, it is at the top of the food chain, and some believe, therefore, that it must contain the most superior nutrition. Even if not, it's certainly the case that any organic life forms coming to the planet will require sustenance, and since all the life forms on Earth will be equally as, well, alien, to the invader's digestive systems, there is perhaps little reason to differentiate between species that contain nutritional value for you.

Presumably if you yourselves are human, you can skip the idea of keeping humans for food. Otherwise, any good farmer knows that the best food – be it fruits, vegetables, fish, poultry or animals, needs to be looked after and husbanded. Different breeds of the same species may have noticeably different flavours and nutritional values. Battery farming is obviously the most cost efficient for large scale processing, but you'll find that properly bred free-range humans are far tastier and more nutritious.

Care And Feeding Of Your Humans

Even so, if terrestrial organisms are edible and nutritious to your species, you would be better off farming and consuming the larger food animals, which have more food on them, and are unable to form organized military resistance groups.

Also, the fact that any organism you can digest can transfer dangerous bacteria to you definitely applies to humans. Eating them will put you at risk of cross-species bacteriological warfare, because it absolutely will not take long before it occurs to the resistance to start infecting themselves in order to introduce harmful bacteria into your food chain. It would be a long game, true, but they may well eventually succeed in causing mass illness among their forces. Since the humans you eat would be being killed anyway, they wouldn't really have anything to lose.

Zoology. You may simply be interested in studying captive specimens, either because this species in particular interests you, or as part of a wider study. It's even possible that your specimens would be valuable to private collections. This is quite inadvisable in general, as you will be spreading a potentially rebellious enemy to several of your locations away from their home, and that will be asking for trouble, as at some point in the future you may face insurrection in many different locations, from the descendants of your specimens, rather than just on Earth.

Medical research. It's always difficult to calculate how useful a study of a species from a completely different biosphere would be in medicine, but there is a common theory among humans that aliens have a particular need to conduct medical experiments on them, as humans conduct experiments on other species on the planet. If your species is carbon-based, then perhaps you have found enough similarities between yourselves and humanity to make such scientific comparisons valuable.

We Will Destroy Your Planet

If this is the case, then you will need to make sure your specimens are suitable for the scientific method – that you have a range of samples, and that they have not been contaminated by your biosphere in any way before the experiment begins. You will also need to maintain a control sample of average, normal (if there is such a thing) humans for comparison.

Whatever the reason for keeping a group of humans around, you will need to be sure that they are healthy and fit for the purpose, and that they are suitably trained and conditioned to accept the situation with equanimity.

FIRST CONTACT

How the humans you encounter when you arrive on Earth will react to you will depend upon a number of varied factors: how human your species is, whether you are openly extraterrestrial or extra-dimensional, how openly hostile you are, how religious the human is, which culture the human is from, and how educated the human is.

In fact, reports and stories about the arrival of visitors from offworld are so much a staple part of human society from its earliest development that it may actually count as an advantage, as the native population is already preconditioned to view such arrivals as relatively normal.

On the downside, most of these tales, especially over the past century or so, have been produced with a rather tribal defensive tone, in which the arriving species are invariably treated as hostile and exploitative. While the reason for this is in fact rooted in human society's past – in which many of their earlier-developing civilizations destroyed or exploited the ones that were less developed – you may find that this all-pervasive image colours the native expectation of you and leads to the belief that you will be attempting conquest, even if you are not.

Care And Feeding Of Your Humans

If you *are* planning a conquest of the Earth, that won't matter, although it may interfere with any plans you have to pretend otherwise as part of a scheme to lull the native authorities into a false sense of security.

It has always been possible that certain types of religiously minded humans would consider you to be gods, angels, demons, or some other form of supernatural entity. This is especially the case if your appearance matches local legends and beliefs about such beings (e.g. you have wings, horns on your forehead, etc), or if you are more geared towards the use of innate natural and biological abilities rather than purely mechanistic technology.

It is obviously best to make your first contact with humans under carefully controlled conditions and ideally well before actually launching your campaign of attack.

In fact, you should be studying them as part of the research phase of your advance planning. Monitor and observe them first, test them, and finally isolate and acquire subjects for testing and interrogation. You may find yourself viewing these subjects simply as lower animals suitable for physical and intelligence testing, to see what kills them, and how they'll react to stimuli, but you should always remember that they are, by some standards, sentient, and so can give you information on their attitudes, plans, and psychology.

Currently, most of the population of Earth, certainly in developed industrialized societies, are perfectly *au fait* with the idea of visitors from other planets and dimensions, thanks to the propaganda called science fiction. Let us make no mistake, much of this type of literature and art is indeed propaganda, telling as it does stories of how almost-invariably hostile aliens are constantly attempting to conquer or destroy the Earth. Even when the stories are about humanity visiting other worlds, they tend to focus on the idea of the aliens found there being evil, and humanity having a duty to try to defeat them, for its own sake.

This is both a blessing and a curse – and may even be a motive, if you've picked up television transmissions from Earth over the past 60 years or so – for those who seek to conquer the planet. It is a blessing because it means the populace have an understanding of the intricacies of space travel, and the fact that they are not the only life in the universe; it is also a curse because it has preconditioned human society and individuals to view alien visitors to the planet as hostile.

This means that establishing trust, however false, in order to leverage surprise, is a much harder job than it might otherwise be. Whether this is actually a deliberate strategy on the part of a media complex in a position (and with a desire) to affect and control the minds of the populace is unclear. There have been other stories released into society that feature friendly or beneficial aliens, so perhaps it is all one big coincidence. If not, then clearly some of you are ahead of the game, as it would make excellent strategic sense in the battle for the hearts and minds of the populace for you to have inserted your own propaganda into the Earth's media, in order to moderate the levels of preprogrammed hostility you might otherwise face.

HOW TO ABDUCT A HUMAN

There are standard protocols for abducting humans from Earth for either interrogation or scientific study. The guidelines are quite simple, and most species should have little difficulty following them. Those of you originating from other time zones or parallel worlds should feel free to follow the same protocols as part of your pre-attack reconnaissance, safe in the knowledge that witnesses and interrogation subjects will assume your actions to have been committed by space travellers.

In particular, the most likely scapegoats will be grey humanoids with large eyes, thought to be from the vicinity of the Zeta II Reticuli star system. Both of these elements actually have purely terrestrial origins (see text box), but in the unlikely coincidental event that any of you *are* large-eyed grey humanoids from the Zeta II Reticuli star system, you will be getting blamed for everybody else's actions, which must be a motive for anger.

Note that if you intend to capture actual humans for interrogation or study as part of a pre-invasion reconnaissance programme, it is not strictly necessary to kill the specimens in order to protect your plans or intentions. In fact, among certain terrestrial societies, the study of random specimens by extraterrestrial visitors is considered a relatively normal occurrence, at least when the typical protocols are followed. Killing them is still the most secure precaution, though, unless you want to fit them with some form of monitoring device, parasite, or mind control apparatus, with which you can use your abductees to learn more during reconnaissance missions, or to conduct operations which you yourself are too nonhuman to get away with.

If you are able to create some sort of duplicate of the test subject – whether it be a robot, clone, plant replica grown in a pod, or some other type of doppelganger, then you should do so, for intelligence-gathering, fifth column duties, and to generally allay suspicion in case, despite your best efforts in selection, they will be missed by someone.

You should look for humans in remote areas, and ones who will not be missed. Hermits, the homeless, individuals on long journeys far from home, and so on.

Firstly, make sure your chosen subject *is*, in fact, a human. Quite apart from the fact that there are many related hominid ape species on the planet, which share a common evolutionary ancestor with humanity, the preponderance of mammalian life in general on the surface of the planet could cause some confusion.

Humans tend to be bipedal and relatively hairless. It's embarrassing enough to have accidentally beamed up an orang-utan or chimpanzee, but there have been many reports from farmers on Earth reporting that their cows and horses have been abducted by aliens. That said, there is also good reason to take sample subjects of other terrestrial species for study. You may wish to compare their biologies, test them as suitable food sources, or even prefer their company to that of more troublesome humans.

Care And Feeding Of Your Humans

Once you have confirmed that your chosen subject is human, and not, for example, a cow, the abduction process should be fairly simple. Since reconnaissance should occur before humanity in general is aware of your presence, isolated individuals should be chosen, to minimize the risk of witnesses or resistance. The subject should be taken either from their sleeping quarters (humans generally sleep singly or in pairs, so these are appropriate numbers) or from a ground vehicle subjected to EMP attack. A small ground vehicle is best, because it again will typically contain one or two humans, and larger vehicles or aircraft will carry with them more danger of witnesses and discovery.

The vehicle approach is recommended. On Earth, only humans will be in control of vehicles, so there is no room for confusion. Simply choose a ground vehicle that is moving in or towards a remote area with no other travellers. Descend in a suitable vessel, stop the vehicle with an EMP burst, and remove the occupants for study.

You should either teleport your abductee into a space vehicle, or carry them there by anti-gravitational means. If you do not have antigravity, then ensuring that the subject is in an altered state of consciousness – by chemical, sonic, or electromagnetic means – will give them the same effect. Your subject should be immobilized but conscious throughout, so that they can respond to our questions, and their brain chemistry responses to different stimuli can be studied without danger of resistance or escape.

All clothing should be removed for separate study. Feel free to poke, prod and probe unnecessarily, as this will be expected. Having chosen a human who will not be missed, you should dispose of them now, or at least ship them to your homeworld or another planet within your sphere of influence where they can be useful in some way.

If it is for some reason important to you to return the subjects, you should replace them in their sleeping quarters or vehicle afterwards. Their complete disappearance will arouse suspicion, and potentially actions against you, but their abduction and return will simply be considered normal, or dismissed as a figment of their imagination.

When you are ready to return your subjects to their sleeping quarters or vehicle, you should take action to suppress their immediate short-term memory, in order to prevent them from either going in to immediate shock, or taking hostile revenge actions. This can be accomplished by either chemical or electromagnetic means. If you are using chemical means, something with a fresh citrus taste will be more readily accepted.

It is quite likely that the subjects will remember the events on a subconscious level, which can be accessed later by hypnosis. This is not undesirable, as you will want to maintain any bond and familiarity that has formed in previous encounters when you return for subsequent studies.

HUMAN RESOURCES

Around 65–70% of the human body is actually water, and the elements that compose it are, in the main, oxygen, carbon, hydrogen, nitrogen, calcium and phosphorus. A total of 20% of the average human is in the form of proteins, and 1–2% lipids, which should make them quite nutritious when freeze-dried.

Carbohydrates are in the form of glycogen and glucose, while other factors include sodium, potassium, amino acids, and fatty acids.

If you do intend to make use of the nutritional value of humans, you must be very sure to keep this fact from them. Any evidence of intent, or documentation to this effect, must be disguised as being intended for other purposes. Recipe files, for example, should be encrypted, perhaps as some form of diplomatic instructions.

VETERINARY CONCERNS

Maintaining the health and fitness of your captives/slaves/subjects on any space voyage, whether to your homeworld or other locations in which you have an interest and a need for humans, is something you will need to think about before initiating any such programme.

The human body is entirely adapted to existence on the Earth's surface, in an upright position, and long-term exposure to microgravity in space has negative effects on it.

In particular, you will find that your humans experience some muscular atrophy and bone decalcification – osteopenia. You will need to ensure your humans maintain an exercise regimen to counteract the muscular atrophy, while mineral supplements and elasticated pressure suits should help compress the limbs and slow the process of osteopenia. Their cardiovascular systems will also slow, as less blood pressure is required to pump blood to the upper parts of the body, and this may affect those who have cardiac arrhythmia.

Almost half of humans – 45% – also suffer from what NASA calls space adaptation syndrome, and is a form of motion sickness caused by the fluids in the inner ear changing distribution. This results in dizziness and vomiting, but fortunately has been observed to last a maximum of 72 hours, and no longer. Nevertheless, you will need to be prepared for cleaning of biohazardous materials.

Other effects and problems your humans may suffer include anaemia – a decrease in red blood cells – fluid redistribution around the fatty tissues of the body, and, doubtless to the embarrassment or amusement of the humans, excess flatulence as gas is redistributed.

All of these problems are purely temporary, and will resolve themselves when the affected human is returned to a surface with stable gravity. Recent research by the Earth's space flight authorities, however, has shown that there may be risks of more permanent damage, in particular to the eyesight, and to some of the brain's pathways. It has recently been suggested that prolonged exposure to microgravity may in fact hasten the development of deteriorative brain conditions such as Alzheimer's disease.

In order to prevent these problems, it is advisable to make sure that the environment on board any transport starships you use is suitable for human cargo/passengers. Ideally, some form of artificial gravity should be used. Failing that, it would be best to house the humans – and, indeed, any other live specimens from Earth, in a rotating section of the ship, in order that centrifugal force should provide the appropriate effects.

Alternatively, try using the rearmost interior bulkheads of your ships as the deck for the human quarters, and make sure to maintain a constant acceleration. Please be aware, however, that launch pressures greater than 3g may prove harmful to those specimens who are particularly young or old, and those who are infirm or injured. It's best to ensure there are upholstered supports and couches for the humans to lie on for takeoff, to avoid spinal and limb damage, and injuries from falls. Launch pressures greater than about 7g will be harmful to all of your specimens, so you must limit your takeoff acceleration.

ALIEN ABDUCTIONS

According to popular myth, aliens have been abducting humans and conducting medical experiments and studies upon them for several decades now.

The first abduction report came from the US in 1961, although there would later be reports of abductions that had supposedly happened earlier. For example, a Brazilian man was supposedly abducted and seduced by an alien temptress in 1956, though the report wasn't made until many year later.

In September of 1961, a couple, Betty and Barney Hill, were driving late one night when they saw a UFO in the sky. They stopped to watch it through binoculars for a while, then continued their journey. At which point, the UFO landed, stopped their car, and several beings took the couple into the ship for medical examinations. The couple forgot all of this at the time, having found themselves further along the road than they remembered driving, but began to remember their experience after having nightmares about it.

When they consulted a hypnotherapist a couple of weeks later, the story came out under hypnosis that they had been abducted by aliens for medical experiments. Among other things, they described the aliens as being grey-skinned, with large wraparound eyes. Betty Hill claimed to remember being shown a star map of the aliens' home planet, and drew a reproduction of it. From this hypnotic regression to unlock what they thought were repressed memories, these two things changed the perception of aliens.

Before the Hill case, the 1950s had seen a fashion for people claiming to have contacted aliens from Mars, Venus and Saturn, who were quite human and friendly, and concerned about Earth's development of nuclear power. These reports of so-called 'contactees' drew on a mix of worry for the future in the post-war atomic era, the burgeoning hippie movement, religion, and carried with a touch of the spiritualist – making contact with intelligences from beyond this world.

We Will Destroy Your Planet

After the Hill case hit the headlines, reports of abductions for medical experimentation by little grey men from Zeta Reticuli flooded the more sensationalist media, and this model became the accepted norm for fictional contact with aliens. Today, this is still the standard form of alien when people report an abduction. But where did it really come from?

In the case of the map, probably just random coincidence. After Betty Hill's drawing of it was published, a primary school teacher from Ohio decided to try to decode it. She assumed that one of the stars on the map must be the Sun, and started making three-dimensional models out of string, comparing arrangements with a star catalogue until she found a match for the line of travel on the map, which she equated to an origin at Zeta II Reticuli. Others have tried the same thing, and generally come up with completely different origin points for the aliens every time, but the Zeta II Reticuli identification stuck in the public consciousness.

As for why the aliens are grey, with large eyes that wrap around to the side of their heads, there are two possibilities. One is that aliens of that nature are visiting the Earth. The other is that the Hills' were subconsciously remembering an alien played by John Hoyt in *The Outer Limits* episode *The Bellero Shield*. This alien appeared in the show right at the time the Hills were having their nightmares, which prompted them to seek hypnosis. The show was in black and white, so the alien was grey, and it was the first alien with wraparound eyes in SF. True, there had been aliens with large black eyes in *Invaders from Mars* in 1953, but those aliens were the then-traditional green, and their eyes were not wraparound.

Since then, the Greys have pretty much sewn up the market for aliens in the developed world (though South America prefers to report hairy dwarves, and lizard-men have always been runners-up), and poor John Hoyt probably never knew what he'd started.

ADDING HUMANS TO YOUR SOCIETY

Rather than eliminating the population of the Earth, a potential option for running the planet – especially if you have a relatively small population, and not really enough people to populate your new property with – is to convert the native population into members of your population. Obviously this will prove easiest if your society is some kind of Empire or Federation made up of many species from different planets – however if your society is heavily into genetic, racial, or cultural purity this will not be an acceptable alternative.

If your society is one made up of multiple species, or indeed is a culture that has been engineered into your present form through choice, then the various kinds of adoption, conversion and assimilation are all viable options.

YOU WILL BE LIKE US

Species that have reached or passed the point of machine-organic singularity may actually require organic components to continue expansion, especially if they have developed to a point beyond organic reproduction. In such an instance, cloned flesh, skin or organs should be a practical consideration for immediate repairs, but if there is a need for a self-sustaining, self-aware and mobile organic component, then humans or other terrestrial animal species may be an appropriate source of new additions.

If your species has reached and passed the point of machine-organic singularity, you may have eschewed natural biological forms of reproduction. In that instance, in order to increase your population to occupy any expansion of territory, it may be necessary to find or create others with that machine-organic singularity.

The human race has not yet reached the point of singularity, and so you may find it necessary to impose that blending of organic and machine by upgrading humanity to incorporate technology alongside biology, in order to assimilate them into your society. This can be attempted in several different ways. Cybernetic enhancements to the physical body can be made by means of surgery, of course, and such procedures to repair physical injury are known and used on Earth already.

There is still the danger of tissue rejecting the implants, of course, and if the subject is not properly psychologically prepared for the replacement of natural body parts with artificial and technological prostheses, problems will arise. Also, simple mechanical prostheses are a long way from integrating the new cyborg into a true post-singularity culture, as they will not have the mental access to the computing power of the society without being able to connect the brain's neuroelectrical function to that of the network as a whole. Nor will the network be able to access the brain, and the organic components will still age and be prone to disease.

You may be seeking to convert humans to a fully artificial form, either entirely cybernetic, as robots, or even entirely digital, as consciousnesses stored in non-physical media. Completely converting humanity into a machine form would perhaps be more a matter of simply uploading the consciousness and mind to a stored digital form and then downloading it into a prepared artificial physical form. This would really just be copying the original mind, however, rather than converting the life form as a whole. On the upside, you could download duplicates of important or valuable personas into whichever form is required.

That being the case, mind you, you could easily populate your new planet with only the best personas, by simply mass-producing bodies to download copies into. That way you can relax and not worry about preserving whole populations, as a dozen or so original personas should be more than enough. You will always, however, have to be on your guard against the possibility of rebellion or revenge from upgraded copies or survivors of a wiped-out humanity.

If your use for the native species of Earth lies along the route of cybernetic conversion, food, or medical use, you might find it less troublesome to keep the human subjects at least sedated, if not in suspended animation. This will reduce the likelihood of insurgency or active resistance.

There are both advantages and disadvantages to this approach. One good thing is that keeping your humans sedated or in a medically induced coma will prevent their physical resistance. They will be unable to deviate from your intentions for them, and you can more precisely control the necessary nutrients or chemical additives that are given to them, by means of intravenous feeds.

There is, however, a downside, especially if you intend them to be used either as a food source or as a work force or organic base to your cybernetic hybrid with machine implants. That downside is muscular atrophy. No matter how good the nutrition, inactivity will cause muscular degradation, which means that they will be less effective as cybernetic organisms or workers, and of less good quality meat, if you're thinking that way.

It's therefore wise, in either case, to allow a certain amount of exercise, to keep your humans at peak fitness for whatever purpose you have in mind for them. In order to limit the chance of resistance, you should probably dose their atmosphere with a light sedative, to keep them docile and non-aggressive.

KEEPING YOUR HUMANS UNDER CONTROL

It should go without saying that whether your human population consists of a few individuals in a cell, or all the peoples of the Earth, you will have to ensure that their behaviour is acceptable to you, and that rebellion is, at the very least, discouraged.

There are many ways to effect control of individuals and populations, ranging from the threat of painful death for the slightest infractions, to rewards of unparalleled treasures for loyalty, with brainwashing and direct telepathic oversight somewhere in between.

Your preference in this regard will depend largely on your attitude to both yourselves and other life forms. Specifically, you will doubtless be more inclined to rule by fear if you have a cultural need to view yourself as superior and more valid life forms. It's easier to mistreat those whom you don't feel quite qualify as a true sentient or civilized species. Fortunately this approach will be well understood on Earth.

BRIBERY AND CORRUPTION

Bribery and corruption are the constant bedfellows of politics and power, and you don't have to have memorized all of the rules and regulations about galactic deal-making and commerce to know that absolutely everyone wants something at some point.

What you can offer the corruptible officials of Earth is surprisingly less obvious. After all, the Earth's currencies and financial systems are in no way related to yours, so you're presumably not going to have terrestrial currency available, and any forms of currency that your society may have will be of no value to the humans you're trying to bribe.

It may be possible for you to acquire terrestrial currency

Care And Feeding Of Your Humans

– either as actual banknotes or as financial data in accounts held on Earth – as part of a pre-landing intelligence-gathering phase. This will obviously be easier to achieve if you yourselves are able to pass for human, or can control human natives in order to make transactions and maintain accounts for you.

If you cannot bribe with currency, then the two real options open to you are to offer either some other form of valuable commodity, such as precious metals, technology, and so on, or else to simply offer actual personal power.

Humans, especially those in positions of authority, are frequently prone to being paid in money – the different forms of tokens of agreed exchange used on Earth – or rewarded by the expansion of their power and influence in return for making certain decisions. It is therefore quite possible that such people in authority can be paid in local currency, or otherwise persuaded to make decisions and instigate policy that benefits your ambitions.

This strategy can be used ahead of a full-scale invasion to, for example, reduce defensive military forces, feed them false information about your plans and capabilities, order military units to be posted away from your landing sites, and so on.

In fact, it is also a strategy suitable for using *instead* of military action. As the legendary military theorist, Sun Tzu, put it, the greatest honour lies in defeating your enemy without fighting him, as if you have to fight then you have already lost the first challenge. This approach is, however, probably less fun. If you're looking to live on Earth long-term either covertly or simply going native, bribery and corruption will be even more important than keeping your human subjects in line.

RELIGION

The use of religion has long been proved an effective method of controlling societies, regardless of the origin of the religion in question.

Religion and its opposites are also excellent ways in which to arrange for different groups of resistance factions to kill each other off, or at least distract each other from the threat your invasion poses. In theocratic and religious-dominated human societies, there has historically been a tendency for secular groups to turn to extremism and violence if they feel persecuted or marginalized. Conversely, in more secular human societies, religious extremism has been prone to violence for exactly the same reasons. Essentially, the group not in power in its society tends to become radicalized against the group in power.

This is worth exploiting as part of your strategy, both before consolidating your takeover, as a part of fragmenting terrestrial defences, and as part of controlling your subjugated populations. It is always resource-efficient – and often amusing and satisfying – to have your enemies weaken and destroy each other, so that the burden of doing so yourself is lessened.

Posing as rival deities or prophets to rival groups should generate conflict between human groups quite quickly and efficiently, but the best era for that in Earth history is past. Most of present-day Earth's societies are sufficiently advanced – remember that humanity has travelled into space already – that it will be unlikely that you can simply pose as gods in order to issue directives. The human populace is aware of the concept of non-divine extraterrestrial life forms, and will not simply assume that your advanced technology is a sign of godhood.

Therefore, the use of religion as a means of control will have to be arranged somewhat more subtly. You will want to have as many humans as possible willing to side with your aims on at least some level. One strategy would simply be to claim to be followers of an existing terrestrial religion, and integrate your policies as you would with any political chain of command.

If you intend to – or insist upon – installing your own native religion as one which humanity should follow, there are three basic strategies you can attempt. The simplest, and least likely to result in a widespread belief system, is to introduce your religion by means of texts and broadcasts, tell the human population about the benefits it offers, and hope that they will take it to heart as they have previously taken so many other religions. Whether this approach succeeds is almost a random gamble; It may or may not appeal, it may come along at the right time or the wrong time, and so on. The second option, of course, is to impose your religion by law and force of arms. Fear of earthly punishments will keep many worshippers in line, and eventually this will transfer itself to belief for many of them. The downside is that strictures imposed from outside tend to spark resentment in both individual humans and in cultures, and this kind of approach is likely to backfire, especially by inspiring those who refuse to follow your belief system to turn to violent resistance.

Historically the best, most successful strategy is actually almost as simple as the first choice, and far less resource-intensive than the second. That is to introduce the religion you wish to use, but to tailor it to the local population, in particular by incorporating structural underpinnings of the pre-existing local religions into your new official religion. For example, notable dates or deities can be adapted, so that the population need only really switch to using your new names and ceremonies for the same things they are already conditioned to understand and go along with.

On a related note, because the Earth is so acquainted with religious conflict throughout its history, there has always been an exploitable connection between religion and military service, with one often using the trappings of the other to attract recruits, or provide a reason for conscription, or an excuse for combat.

This can be useful for your rule of humanity, if you want to recruit local auxiliaries to serve in your forces, or any other form of service that works best with willing volunteers. Making assisting you an act of religious devotion to whichever deities your humans believe in will make many of them want to serve you, and completely shun the idea of resistance or rebellion.

DIRECT MIND CONTROL

If you have the ability to directly affect the thoughts and feelings of others purely by the power of your mind, then feel free to do so. You will need a constant rota of able telepaths and empaths to do this, however, depending on how many human minds each can affect. If your telepaths can influence or affect many human minds, then a few in each region might be able to do the job. However, if it's only a one-to-one ratio, then you'll need at least as many of you as there are humans – and probably more, because your telepaths will need to rest at times, and someone will have to pick up the slack when they do.

Alternatively, you can get the same effect by using the media to direct human culture. This is how Earth governs itself anyway, so you would be able to adapt the current system with the minimum of fuss, by having the messages you want placed into entertainments and news releases. This principle has been used effectively for thousands of years, and is sometimes referred to as the 'bread and circuses' approach, as this is how it was implemented by the historic Roman Empire. Avoid the temptation to try inserting your propaganda into subliminal tones or images, however – research on Earth has shown that, although there is a popular belief that these work, they in fact do not, but instead simply irritate. Openness or subtext are the best approaches.

Finally, the simplest means of mass control is chemical. Introduce relaxants into the atmosphere or water supplies, and you will find that populations in the affected areas are far more docile and happy to go along with your directions for society. The small percentage who are immune to the effect or find a way to avoid exposure to the chemicals can be dealt with in other ways – either hunted down and eliminated, or bribed, or otherwise brought to heel.

Likewise, parasitism can offer direct control over the

human mind, though this will certainly require a population equal to the human population. If your species is a type of intelligent parasite, then you must be able to link with humans in great numbers.

If you are few, you will have to adapt one of the other strategies along with the direct control of your human host. That is to say, you can directly control your host, but must use that host as a proxy through which to control a wider group of humans by means of bribery, religion, or whichever other means suits your society and purpose.

BREEDING FROM YOUR HUMANS

Yes, this happens too.

You will find that if you wish to maintain a collection of humans, or a workforce, you will have to ensure that they continue to produce further generations of humans. This is a simple enough matter – so long as you ensure that there are at least 50 breeding pairs to maintain genetic diversity, they'll take care of the matter themselves. The population of the Earth will continue as per usual.

There is also, however, the issue of breeding from humans and yourselves.

Much of humanity's concerns about the possibility of conquest seem to centre around the desire of the *invaders* to mate with human women and produce alien-human hybrids. In fact, any subjects you abduct for interrogation or testing will almost certainly assume that this is the purpose of their abduction. Conversely, much human thought has also gone into the idea of seducing extraterrestrial females, should the opportunity occur.

Thankfully (or unfortunately, if your expedition to Earth is being arranged with this in mind) this is pretty much impossible, at least without a lot of genetic manipulation, and if you're going to go around building genomes from individual chromosomes and genes, all artificially put together, then you may as well just build your desired life form and save yourself the bother of mounting an expensive military campaign.

Humans, as visitors to the planet since at least medieval times have noticed and recorded, are not split into different species, but are separated into two distinct forms on a gender basis. They are generally easily distinguishable. The males tend to be sturdier with greater upper body strength, while the females have finer hair, and a thorax of a different construction.

These differences are due to the species – like most of the animal species on the planet – having a relatively crude and inefficient primary and secondary reproductive system, which relies on the male implanting the female with one set of DNA, while her body provides a second set and combines them into a new human. As mammals, humans give live birth and do not lay eggs.

For some reason, humans familiar with the concept of alien life have long displayed a fear and fascination for the idea of that alien life attempting to intervene in the reproductive cycle, usually by seeking to replace the human male in the act of providing DNA. This may well lead to some misunderstandings when you encounter humans, regardless of your actual intentions towards them. This fear is probably tribal in origin, but, where extraterrestrials are concerned, it is a fear reliant upon ignorance of how DNA works – or even what it actually is.

DNA is essentially a set of instructions to a mother life form of how to create a next generation life form: what chromosomes to put where (determining gender), what to make the cells out of, and where to put each one, and so forth.

Humans have an average of about a hundred trillion cells in their body, each containing a nucleus made of a molecule called, on Earth, DNA, or deoxyribonucleic acid. In purely chemical terms, the molecule is made of two strands twisted together, of a combination of only four chemicals (adenine, cytosine, thymine and guanine). These chemicals are paired off into links (base pairs) that join the two strands together. Three billion of these base pairs make up a DNA molecule, but the molecule is more than just a chemical lump. This is what humans tend not to understand; the sequence is a coded instruction.

Specifically it is a chemical programme that instructs a female human's body in how to construct a new human. Obviously the programme, like any software, can only be run on hardware that can interpret the instructions, and there are limits to this. Species on Earth can only interpret the instructions for their own species, or at least related species from the same genus. This would also be the case with alien invaders and humans – the DNA from the male would have to be re-coded in such a way that the mother's body, of whichever species, is capable of interpreting the instructions.

This is all a problem even without asking the simple question of why a nonhuman would be attracted to a human anyway, since – at least on Earth – the reproductive urge and triggers are hardwired in at a biological level. Species are designed to mate with their own species, to propagate that species. On the other hand, if humans fall within your definition of beauty regardless of the biology, then recreational interaction should actually be quite safe, if potentially falling foul of planetary and galactic obscenity laws.

But, if you really want to be shown some of that Earth thing called kissing, it's really going to depend on how human-like you yourselves look, as humans on the whole are known to be very parochial. Not to mention fussy and more concerned with outward appearance than inner magnificence.

COLLATERAL DAMAGE

It is always possible that your interest in Earth has little or nothing to do with either its people or resources, but as a factor in galactic politics and overall strategy. In other words, you may be mostly concerned with the planet's – or the whole system's – strategic position in relation to both your own home planet or civilization, and other species and civilizations with whom you must deal.

Perhaps the Earth is in a vital location through which several trade routes pass, or would be a source of vital resources for an enemy you're at war with. Such situations are many and varied, and all require measured and thoughtful responses.

RENDERING THE PLANET UNUSABLE

If the issue you face is one of the physical structure and presence of the Earth being of value to an enemy but not to yourself, then the obvious solution is to remove the Earth.

We Will Destroy Your Planet

This is the obvious solution, but, as we've already seen, not the simplest or easiest one. The Earth is, after all, very difficult to destroy. If you are unwilling or unable to destroy the planet, a number of possible solutions to this strategic problem present themselves.

The trick, then, is to remove it from play by other means.

Hiding the planet will be the first potential means to keep it out of enemy hands. If you have the ability to cloak your ships with any form of stealth technology, then up-scaling this technology to cloak the planet as a whole is an option to try. The energy requirements would surely be enormous, but your enemies will be unable to land on the Earth and exploit it for their own desires if they can't find it.

The practical problems with such an approach of this nature is that the planet's location would still be noticeable through the effect of its mass on the rest of the system, and its size and position could be calculated from its gravitational effects on the Sun, Mars and Venus. In essence, therefore, you'd have to somehow cloak, camouflage, or otherwise hide the entire Solar system. This could probably be done by constructing a Dyson sphere around it − a shell that would absorb all the energy of the Sun before it could escape into interstellar space, but, again, the mass of such an object would still be noticeable. Sadly, there's too much risk that a gravitational mass that can't be seen or identified, but can be detected, might be more likely to attract attention from the curious.

The other potential downside to rendering a planet invisible is the danger of a ship crashing into it before noticing that it was there.

Distraction is another option. Positioning gravitational masses outside the Solar system could be used to create gravitational lensing when seen from the viewpoint of a specific approach or enemy. This would bend light around the gravitational mass, which would make the Sun and/or

Collateral Damage

the Earth appear to be in a different location, or cast false images of it in addition to the genuine article. This wouldn't really be worth the effort, though, as any astrophysicist or starship navigator worthy of the name would be able to run the calculations to reveal the true location of the actual object.

Playing tricks with time is another option. If you have the ability to manipulate time, through whatever means, and are able to affect the entire planet – which would mean everything within a certain distance from the centre of the planetary mass out to a point in the gravity well beyond the atmosphere – you can shift the Earth out of temporal phase with the rest of the universe. In essence, you could make it always a few seconds ahead of the rest of the universe. The presence of the planet would be as detectable as ever, but it couldn't be approached, attacked, or landed upon.

To do this might require increasing the planetary mass to something like that of a neutron star or even a black hole, however, and no science as yet known could fulfil the task.

The other problem with shifting the planet slightly out of time is that the inability of anything to transition between the planet's time zone and the rest of the universe would extend to your own ships, so you would no longer be able to use it yourself, and any of your forces left there would be trapped. Nevertheless, if you simply want to get the Earth out of the way for your enemies, this would do it.

Whether you can render the Earth unusable for your enemies depends on what they might want to use it for. If they want organic resources on the surface, then a pathogen inimical to all carbon-based life should remove it nicely.

If they require the liquid water on the surface, that's a bigger deal. Heating the planet would create a more destructive cycle of weather and rain, but the water would still, overall, be there. The same would apply to extinction-level meteor bombardment.

We Will Destroy Your Planet

To get rid of the Earth's water in all its forms – liquid, ice, and in the atmosphere – your best hope will be to blow up the Sun. Causing the Sun to reach the stage of its life and fusion processes in which it will expand into a red giant star will strip away the Earth's atmosphere and boil off the oceans. This will leave the planet as a sterile rock, and, if necessary, you can still mine or garrison that in order to be completely sure that no rivals will exploit your conquest.

STRATEGIC AREA DENIAL

If you have neither the technology nor the inclination to carry out such actions as moving the planet through time, or blowing up the Sun, then you will be looking at the matter of strategic area denial.

Area denial is a discipline on both strategic and tactical levels, which requires its own specialist weaponry and units. The aim of area denial is very simple – as the name implies, it means denying a particular area to others. This does not necessarily mean destroying the area. It can as easily mean making it less attractive to an enemy, or making it more trouble to gain than is worth the effort of doing so.

An area denial weapon is one designed to prevent others from entering, conquering, or acquiring a particular strategic or resource-rich environment. Obvious area denial weapons, for smaller areas on the surface, are things like land mines, or automated turret guns that fire upon anything that trips a built-in motion detector. These types of weapons are ideal for guarding limited areas such as military facilities, or landing areas – though turret guns have the problem of running through ammunition very quickly and then needing to be visited to be rearmed. As such they're actually better used as a kind of hostile alarm, more to alert your forces to respond, than simply as a defensive measure in their own right.

Collateral Damage

One simple way of making the planet less attractive to your enemies is just to get it yourself first. Your enemies will not come to Earth and try to strip it of resources if they know you have already shipped all that valuable booty back home. They will be less likely to try to moving in and colonizing if they know you are already in residence.

If you have no real interest in occupying the planet or using its resources for yourself, then the best way to make it less attractive or too much trouble to others is to make their operations impossible, due to local conditions. The second best way is to scare them off, so that they will not have the motive or willingness to approach the Earth. Rather conveniently, these two methods of discouragement can be combined with the application of a particular type of area denial weapon: Biowarfare.

Specifically, the creation and use of actual life forms as biological/area denial weapons.

USING LIFE FORMS AS WEAPONS

Plague is the first choice for keeping a whole planet out of bounds. In essence, area denial weapons quarantine a region from approach by your enemies and rivals, or potential enemies and rivals. That word quarantine, however, can also imply cutting off a region to prevent disease from spreading into or out of it, and that's an obvious inspiration.

An area denial pathogen would of necessity be different than a pathogen designed for cleansing a smaller region of a range of native life forms. The latter type of biological agent ideally needs to be short-lived, requiring incubation in the cells of the target species to survive. Once the targeted life forms are dead, such a virus or bacterium should die out, allowing your forces to take over the cleansed area with impunity.

We Will Destroy Your Planet

If, however, you want to make an area inhospitable, and tainted with a pathogen that will affect any visitors at any point over an unknown length of time, then you need a longer-lasting biological weapon. This can be in the form of bacterial or viral spores capable of returning to viability from dormancy after long periods. If you are merely denying one area on an otherwise occupied Earth – say you want to keep a particular island free of life, but with native life remaining in other locales – then such a disease spore is a reasonable option, so long as it is quick-acting, and cannot be carried by winds to inhabited areas.

To deny a whole planet to anyone else out there, however, is a different type of problem. A disease will only affect types of life that are either native to the planet it came from, or that it has been engineered to attack. Since you do not necessarily know which other visitors will try to take the Earth, you will have to engineer something that responds to chemical elements in organic form, rather than to a specific type of cells from a single world. Making a bacterium that attacks a specific form of an element means that it will not only attack extraterrestrial visitors, but even their ships and equipment.

Biological warfare involving bacteria and pathogens is one thing, but it is also worth considering the use of more complex life forms as weapons, especially with regard to the concept of area denial.

Parasitic organisms are frequently considered to be good area denial weapons. For example, you can seed the planet with a genetically engineered pupal stage, which will hibernate until disturbed by the presence – chemical spoor, body heat, pheromones, for example – of a visitor. Your pupal life form can then attack a newcomer, convert the intruder biomass into a chrysalid stage for itself, and then emerge as a life form that can produce new pupal life forms to repeat the cycle. Insect societies are a good model for this, and your full adult parasite forms can be designed with appropriate weapons and reactions – claws, fangs, venom, acid, or whatever your preference.

Collateral Damage

A lack of a human population may be suspicious to other species, perhaps even others than the one whom you are trying to prevent from taking over the Earth, especially if they have been conducting long-term reconnaissance of their own. It's also possible that you may want to eliminate human life without getting into trouble with authorities elsewhere, who may be keeping an eye on things. Therefore, if you wish to turn the Earth into a human-free deathtrap it would be prudent to make everything seem as normal as possible on the planet.

For this, you need a type of biological weapon that can pass for human. You need to infiltrate such weapons on to the planet, where they may begin to replicate and replace humans with more of themselves. The perfect example of such an organism would be the one known on Earth from John W. Campbell Jr's *Who Goes There?*, best remembered in its screen incarnation as John Carpenter's movie *The Thing*. This is the perfect biological weapon to act as both a destroyer and an area denial weapon. It exists purely to absorb, copy, and infect the cells of other life forms, replacing them with its own. A computer on screen in the film suggests that the entire population of the Earth would have been infected within 27,000 hours – about 3.08 years. Since the organism has been frozen in the ice for thousands of years and is still active, it would remain there once the Earth's indigenous life forms (all mammals at least, as it impersonates both humans and canines during the film) were extinct. This would mean no one else dare land on the Earth, and the planet would remain a quarantined plague world, useless to anyone.

Likewise, if you have an engineered weapon that simply absorbs and replicates the human form and memories, but does not need any inbuilt weapons or hostility, you need only make sure the organism is sterile, and cannot reproduce in human form or manner. Within the lifespan of the youngest human replaced, the planet would become a ghost world, no longer inhabited.

We Will Destroy Your Planet

The more hostile previous type of organism, however, would be the better bet for remaining viable as a trap or deterrent. So long as it can hibernate until disturbed, the whole cycle can begin again each time someone attempts to visit the infected planet.

The greatest advantage to any form of engineered bioweapon which infects or absorbs those who come into contact with it is that every attacker or intruder who attempts to trespass within the denied area protected by such an organism will not only be prevented from doing so, but will actually add to the defences and make them stronger.

GARRISONING THE PLANET

Establishing a military garrison on the planet may be necessary, if you're looking to prevent activity by other civilizations in the vicinity.

It may not in fact be necessary to conquer the Earth in order to establish a garrison there. In fact, it may not even be desirable to do so. This is one of those situations in which simply making peaceful overtures to terrestrial authorities may well achieve the result you want.

This is because, since humans are already quite preconditioned to accept the idea of hostile forces among the stars, it should be a relatively simple matter to establish that your enemies are bent on the conquest of the Earth. With careful manipulation of the collective psyche it should even be possible to persuade human forces to form the bulk of your garrison, risking their lives under your guidance so that your forces don't have to. Aside from negating the need to conquer the Earth, this also has the advantage of sparing your forces for more important duties elsewhere.

If you want to be sure of conducting your own security according to your own protocols and strictures, however, you can certainly conquer the Earth to establish a garrison. If you do, you will have to guard it against local resistance, and you will risk the chance of your rival conquerors allying themselves with the human population, who know the planet better than you do. If you follow this route, you will therefore have to choose between the potential options of using the human population as cannon-fodder or living shields and setting up your garrisons and launch sites as far from the local populace as possible, in order to avoid sabotage and resistance.

Keeping other space travellers and would-be planetary conquerors away from the Earth is something you will have to think about even if you do not know of any enemy plans to exploit the planet.

PROTECTING YOUR ILL-GOTTEN GAINS

In an ideal universe, once you've conquered the Earth, you'd happily build your palaces or garrisons, and wallow in piles of whatever your idea of treasure is, while humanity worships you as gods, and live (if you're organic, and not a machine civilization) happily ever after.

Nobody ever said this is an ideal universe. If *you* are out to conquer the Earth, it must be pretty likely that there are others who will also be doing likewise. That means that other species – who hopefully will also be referring to this guide – will be viewing *you* as the hapless defenders of the planet.

DEFENDING THE EARTH

It goes without saying that you don't want this chapter to fall into human hands.

You cannot rely on human detection or early warning systems or their defences. After all, they didn't manage to stop you. There are early warning systems in place to detect Near-Earth Objects, natural bodies such as asteroids and comets, which may pose a threat to the planet. These systems have allegedly detected over 90% of the regular objects that come close to Earth, but are not so good at detecting individual rogue objects passing through the system just the once. In fact, those humans who run this detection programme have been known to acknowledge that there would be only two or three minutes' warning of such a natural impactor. Obviously, the chances of detecting an incoming supraluminal object, such as a starship, are very much less than zero.

Collateral Damage

In order to detect approaching vessels, you would be best to put your detection and early warning technologies in neighbouring star systems, always assuming you have the faster than light technology to allow the detection stations to alert you on Earth to anything they detect. There won't be much point in noticing an invasion fleet passing by Proxima Centauri at several times light speed, if you won't get the message for four years.

For those wondering, the ten closest stars to Earth are Proxima Centauri (4.2 light years), Alpha Centauri A and B (4.3 light years), Barnard's Star (5.9 light years), Wolf 359 (7.7 light years, and reportedly a good spot to muster a fleet to defend Earth in the 24th Century), Lalande 21185 (8.26 light years), Sirius A and B (8.6 light years), Lutyen 726-8 A and B (8.73 light years), Ross 154 (9.94 light years), Ross 248 (10.32 light years) and Epsilon Eridani (10.5 light years), which is the closest known extra solar system with at least one planet.

Closer to the Earth, you ought to seed the Oort cloud – the dust and gases remaining from the creation of the Solar system – with detectors, especially ones that will detect gravitational disturbances and variances in mass. The asteroid belt between Mars and Jupiter is deceptive, and would not make as good a setting for sensors as you might expect. This is because gravitational and centrifugal forces have caused it to form a relatively flat belt, as an orbit in the plane of the ecliptic, like the other planets. It would be better to distribute an array of sensors and detectors in a spherical formation around the solar system, since there is no guarantee – or even likelihood – that any space travellers would enter the system on the plane of the ecliptic, from outer planets to inner.

After the problem of detecting approaching rivals or authorities, the next order of business will be for you to actually prevent your rivals from attacking or landing on your newly conquered Earth.

We Will Destroy Your Planet

Minefields might work against incoming starships, if the mines are close enough together to provide good coverage. Again, however, this would require englobing the entire planet, and at a distance further out from the surface than any effects from detonation could reach. That would require an incredible amount of mines, bearing in mind that you will need to put them around in all dimensions, not just a belt around the plane of the ecliptic, as most proposed minefields in terrestrial fiction would have it.

The requirements could be worse, mind you. As you may have seen in the *Blake's 7* transmission *Star One*, the fictional Terran Federation in that series proposed having a minefield protecting the entire galaxy from incursion from the neighbouring Andromeda Galaxy. Disappointingly, this particular media entry seemed to believe that simply having a patch of mines at one spot at the edge of the galaxy would do the job, with no suggestion that the extragalactic invaders could simply go over, under, or around the field.

This, in fact, doesn't occur to the invaders either, indicating that they're not really suited for the job.

It's also debatable whether minefields would be of any help against vessels jumping from one point in space-time to another through an intermediate alternate medium such as hyperspace. Obviously a minefield is no barrier to wormhole travel either, or any form of matter transmission. Nor are such types of travel likely to be detected by any sensor array in either the Solar or neighbouring systems.

The best way to keep anyone from physically landing on the planet would be a force shield of some kind that completely englobes the planet – but it had better be damn strong, as mass-driven asteroids would make really good battering rams. Your other option is to use surface-based weaponry to try to destroy motherships in orbit, and shoot down invasion craft as they descend.

To protect against incoming wormhole or matter

transmission signals, you ought to be looking at that which would disrupt the signal. It is always possible to affect wormholes by the use of gravity, which is a useful way to sabotage attempts to send information, data, or physical reinforcements or equipment to Earth by such means. Likewise the wormholes would also affect gravity.

Some physicists believe that a navigable wormhole would require asymptomatically 'flat' space for a huge distance around it, and thus mean that the entrances and exits would have to be situated far away from any noticeable gravity wells, and perhaps even outside the Roche limit of a star. (If you pick up some holiday reading on Earth, you'll find this limitation in the works of Iain M. Banks.) Some have even suggested similar limits for being able to warp space around a ship, or access hyperspace.

In terms of non-navigable wormholes which could carry data – or even the data required to reintegrate a teleported object – there are some more interesting developments to consider, in any defence against the like. For one thing, it is now known on Earth that there is a set of what NASA calls 'X-points' or 'electron diffusion regions' – essentially direct pathways – connecting the upper atmosphere of the planet with the surface of the Sun. These regions act as portals, giving uninterrupted links from one to the other, and causing heating and geomagnetic storms on Earth – but they surely also offer obvious possibilities as to diverting unwanted intruders who attempt to interfere with your conquest.

Defending against temporal incursions is a trickier matter, as gravity strong enough to warp space-time will be at least as dangerous to the planet and your occupying forces as to any attempt to travel through time. This fact does offer a detection method, thankfully, and observation of local gravity fluctuations around the globe can be used as a handy indicator of where potential temporal fluctuations or incoming time-shifts may occur.

We Will Destroy Your Planet

Observation of the populace will be your other main way of spotting any time travellers, who may be equipped with temporally inappropriate clothing or technology. Even if they come from the future, inaccurate records may have led them to carry equipment from a slightly earlier period, or the wrong geographical context.

A fetish for telephone booths is another indicator, and, as it happens, the most disturbing one. In the event of encountering such a traveller, run. Just run.

Defending against visitors from parallel universes or alternate dimensions will be just as difficult, as they may be effectively indistinguishable from your own forces. In fact they may, from their point of view, *be* your forces. They may even be you!

Such visitors are more likely to attempt to infiltrate your own operations by stealth, replacing your own versions of you. Depending upon your society's collective psychology and motivation, this may not actually count as a counter-conquest, if you happen to share a common goal.

The most practical problem will occur if you are visited by invaders from some kind of anti-matter dimension, in which case the problem will both announce itself, and almost certainly solve itself, by explosive means.

DEFENSIVE WEAPONS

As it stands, the Earth still has no effective defensive weapons to protect against spaceborne incursion or assault, therefore you will have to install your own that you have brought with you for the purpose, or, more sensibly, build them locally to a standard design.

The simplest and quickest form of defensive weaponry you will be able to install is the missile, of course, and there are many suitable launch sites around the globe, which you

Collateral Damage

can rebuild (having destroyed them during your attack). If you have conquered or gained influence by mind control, bribery, or alliance with human military organizations, you should be able to easily negotiate use of suitable launch sites and human support crews. Humanity has a great deal of experience in the use of ballistic and orbital rocket launches, and will require little if any retraining to perform these duties for you. If you have negotiated your rule, then treason and resistance should not be a serious problem either, though it always pays to be careful. If you have conquered the Earth by hostile means, you will be better off taking sole control of the launch sites, and maintaining high security around them so that resistance fighters don't use them on your ships.

Energy weapons of whatever variety are always a good idea, if you can target them quickly and accurately enough. This is more of a problem when using them from a surface position against the sky as a whole, because you are now aiming out away from an obvious focus point, while your attackers will be able to focus on your more limited position.

On the positive side, most forms of energy beam, such as lasers, microwave beams, and so on, are not in the visible spectrum, especially in vacuum. (Humans may not realize this, as their visual depictions of such weapons use artistic licence to make them colourful.) This means that attacking spacecraft will not be alerted to your shots until they actually hit something, while you, being based in an atmosphere, will have more chance of seeing where their shots are going, as they disrupt water vapour, and so on.

As experienced planetary conquerors, you will doubtless by now be aware that the best place to defeat any attack on the planet is in orbit, or even beyond – basically, before the enemy can actually reach the surface of the planet.

Mines in high orbit are a simplistic type of defensive weapon, but far better than mines are singularities, if they can be placed safely without threatening your own operations.

We Will Destroy Your Planet

Singularities, or some other form of gravitational attractor, will efficiently draw enemy ships off course, and potentially cause them to crash. Setting high-velocity debris into orbit around such an attractor – or indeed into any area of space that you expect to be interrupted by unwanted visitors – will add an effective disabling tool.

As with letting gravity do the work in bombarding the Earth with meteors, you do not need to construct sophisticated and resource-intensive weapons and booby-traps to take out enemy ships when any old rubbish you don't need any more, if it's moving fast enough, will do at least as much damage.

Put simply, though, the best way for you to defend your new world is to have your ships posted in a picket formation around the system, ready to engage any interlopers who come to try to steal your prize away from you.

NO BATTLE PLAN SURVIVES FIRST CONTACT WITH THE ENEMY

No planetary conquest goes without a hitch, either. The business of conducting a military campaign is incredibly complex, dangerous, and requires astronomical time and energy devoted to making sure that attacks, strategies and logistics all come together to carry a force forward to ultimate victory. The business of travelling away from your homeworld, hurling your fragile bodies into the stars with no idea of what you might find there, while handling all the formulae of mathematics and science necessary to travel to a whole other world, is immensely and insanely complex. The business of understanding and interacting with species so alien to your own, and correctly interpreting how they live is another massively difficult demand.

Invading the Earth combines all of those stupendous difficulties, and multiplies them. The complexity and difficulty increases exponentially with each requirement. It is therefore inevitable that things will go wrong at some point.

You must understand this. There is no such thing as a flawless campaign, and it is not a matter of *if* something goes wrong, but *when* and *what* will go wrong. Overconfidence in your racial or cultural superiority will be a far bigger threat to your campaign than anything that the human resistance forces will be able to throw at you. You must understand that this is a fact, because when you understand that, you will be able to accept it, and deal with it. That is when you'll be able to recover from such failures and setbacks.

There is a tale told on Earth about a warrior named Miyamoto Musashi, who lived in 16th and 17th century Japan, and was regarded as that culture's greatest warrior. One day a farmer came to him and asked his advice. The farmer had been challenged to a duel by another renowned and deadly warrior, and had accepted rather than be seen as a coward and killed anyway. The farmer was no warrior, so he asked Musashi what he should do. Musashi told him, 'Firstly, accept that you will die tomorrow.' Then he showed the farmer to hold his sword above his head, and said, 'When he kills you, bring your sword straight down on his head, and he will die with you.'

Not exactly reassured, the farmer went to the site of the duel and took up the position Musashi had shown him. When the fearsome challenger arrived, he drew his sword and made to kill the farmer, but then held back at the last moment. He studied the farmer's position, and paced around him. All day he paced, occasionally trying to find an angle that would result in him killing the farmer without dying himself. At sunset, he threw down his sword in disgust and walked away.

No Battle Plan Survives First Contact With The Enemy

The farmer had won his duel by accepting that it could only go wrong. So you must accept that something will always go wrong. And always expect the unexpected, because that is what will happen.

IN THE EVENT OF A CRASH LANDING

Unfortunately, no matter how experienced the pilot, or how advanced and/or reliable the technology, things do sometimes go wrong, even without enemy action to cause it. Storms, solar flares, collision with other craft, and simple wear and tear are all possible reason for one of your ships to crash on Earth, killing or stranding any occupants. Whatever the circumstances of such an incident, you will have to take steps to minimize the damage it will do to your plans.

We Will Destroy Your Planet

If the accident occurs before your presence is known, you must act immediately to prevent it from giving away the fact that you are taking an interest in the Earth. This is the case regardless of the size of the ship that crashed. Ideally, you should always have a search and rescue plan prepared for any expedition that visits the planet. All ships and individuals should have homing equipment that will lead a rescue mission – but not the humans – to them. Emergency life-support systems should be available for all occupants of your craft.

If your intentions are peaceful, or at least stealthy, or if you have reason not to mind whether or not the local authorities know that you are visiting the planet, then it may be in your interest to ask for their assistance. It will be in their immediate interests to give their help, if only to help quarantine the site in case of any biological contamination, or to prevent the populace at large from finding out about you under uncontrolled conditions.

If your intentions are hostile, you should ensure that all your vessels that enter the atmosphere are fitted with remote-controlled self-destruct systems, so that if the craft should prove impossible to recover, it can at least be destroyed in order to prevent it from being captured and reverse-engineered by human scientists. Additionally, it is wise to make sure that there are multiple systems in place to wipe any onboard computer memory and navigational data. All the occupants should have a means of doing so, there should be an automated system, and you should be able to trigger such a memory wipe remotely. This is very important because you will not want the indigenous population – soon to be the resistance – to gain access to your scientific knowledge, tactical and strategic plans, weapons details, or (especially if there's a chance of the ship being repaired or reverse-engineered by them) the location and directions to your homeworld. You do not want humanity being able to bring a revenge war to you.

No Battle Plan Survives First Contact With The Enemy

If the crash is of a small ship, such as a scout vessel small enough to go unnoticed or at least undiscovered for a little while, you should send a recovery ship to attempt to remove the downed vessel from the planet. Aside from not wanting to let humans capture it, every piece of logistical equipment is incredibly valuable when you are so far from home, and it may be reparable back home, or aboard a mothership with proper engineering facilities.

If the crashed vessel cannot be recovered, it should be destroyed, either by shipboard weapons on the rescue vessel, demolition charges fitted by your recovery team, or the onboard self-destruct system you should have installed. If your intentions are hostile, and the humans have noticed the crash, your stealth plan is blown, and you should begin your asteroid bombardment immediately.

In the event of the crash of a large ship, one big enough not to go unnoticed, or which does major damage to a terrestrial population centre, then if there are no survivors you should either begin an immediate attack before human resistance can be mustered, or simply leave the planet, your chances blown.

If there are survivors, you may try to rescue them, but, again, beginning an attack would be the most sensible option at this point, especially if the survivors are troops or are aware that you are planning an attack. Any survivors who fall into human hands may, however long it takes for translation and contextual understanding to be developed, give up vital information about your forces, your society, and your plans.

The occupants of your craft should be trained in escape and evasion techniques before ever being allowed to pilot a vessel into Earth's atmosphere. Even if your plans are not overtly hostile, your personnel should be prepared to hide as much as possible, and avoid detection by native civilians and the terrestrial authorities, because, unless your species can pass as human, they may provoke a hostile response from surprised natives, however unintentional that hostility.

Depending on your species' appearance, they may frighten or repulse the natives, and humans have a tendency to respond to fear with hatred and aggression rather than rational thought. It's also equally possible that your pilots may not even be recognized as an alien species, and harmed by mistake or misidentification.

Before any descent into the atmosphere, suitable rendezvous points should be agreed with other units, and your search and rescue teams made aware of those locations. That way, stranded pilots can make their way towards a location at which there is a much greater chance of being quickly found by a rescue ship, and picked up.

If you are not already in conflict with humanity, and especially if they are unaware of your presence and interest in their world, your downed personnel should avoid all contact with humans, if at all possible. If, however, you are already in open conflict, then it can be left up to the individual pilot to determine whether to take hostile action on the ground if targets of opportunity present themselves.

If you do not recover or destroy a downed ship in time to prevent its capture, then you should at the very least ensure that all its systems are wiped and shut down. Once it has been installed at a human military or scientific facility, the facility should be taken out with a meteor strike. This will destroy both the captured vessel and the human scientists learning too much about it, as well as preventing that facility's further use in reverse-engineering other technology captured from you. If you are not yet in open conflict with humanity, this meteor strike can be made as part of an overall bombardment or left as a single incident, which the humans will attribute to natural causes.

ACCIDENT BLACKSPOTS

Over the past century or so, there have been several reported crashes of alien vessels on the Earth. Although none have yet been proven to be the demise of extraterrestrial craft – quite the opposite, in fact – they have become ingrained in human culture as proof of the concept that such things can happen.

LAKE BAIKAL, TUNGUSKA, SIBERIA: On 30 June 1908, an object exploded south of Lake Baikal, the largest body of fresh water on Earth. The blast has been estimated to be in the ten to fifteen megaton range, well capable of flattening a city if it had struck one. As it is, the airburst 5 miles high flattened something like 800 square miles of forest below. Although scientists today are pretty much convinced that the object was a comet fragment, it did not take that long for speculation about an artificial origin to begin.

Witness statements described the course taken by the object in the sky. It turns out that the object changed direction several times, before heading towards Lake Baikal and exploding. This led Soviet scientist Alexander Kazantsev to suggest in a book, *Burning Island*, in 1946 that the object may have been spacecraft in trouble, heading for a source of fresh water. He suggests that the ship was nuclear powered, hence the apparent atomic blast when it finally gave up the ghost.

Many subsequent writers, both in Ufology and science fiction, have followed up on this idea, ensuring that it remains one of the most popular theories about the event today. Most of these theorists, however, are simply convinced by Kazantsev being a scientist, and are unaware that the book *Burning Island* is a science fiction novel, and that he became an SF writer alongside being an engineer.

We Will Destroy Your Planet

NEW MEXICO: This US State is, at least according to Ufologists, a full-on accident black spot for flying saucers and alien craft in general, with no less than three famous cases in a relatively small area.

The most famous is the Roswell case, in which the then US Army Air Force announced that a flying disc had crashed on a ranch 75 miles from the town of Roswell during a thunderstorm in early July 1947. The Air Force was then forced to make an embarrassing apology, claiming the flying saucer was really a weather balloon. They've since spent the past 60 years coming up with occasional new explanations for what the Roswell object was. This is counterproductive, as it just means everyone who has followed the story will never believe the current version.

Although modern believers tend to associate the crash at Roswell with the recovery of alien bodies – the 'Grey' types that began to become prominent after the Betty and Barney Hill abduction case in 1961 – this was never actually a part of the original 1947 reports, but was added to the mythology in the 1970s by writer and part-time CIA prankster, William Moore. The US Air Force has done itself no favours in recent years by buying into this later retroactive continuity, and trying to explain away the bodies in their more recent Roswell case reports.

It is most likely that the Roswell object was a different type of balloon, one of Project Mogul's high-altitude observation balloons designed to monitor the upper atmosphere for signs of Soviet nuclear tests. This project actually belonged to the US Navy, and, due to compartmentalization of information for security reasons, the Air Force at the time was completely unaware of it, hence their original confusion.

That said, the evidence has long since disappeared, so we will never know for sure. However, if it was a genuine alien craft that crashed, it is ironic that something designed to cross interstellar space and survive the heat of atmospheric re-entry should be downed by a mere thunderstorm.

So, where did the idea of there being alien bodies come from?

Actually, from another reported crash shortly afterwards, at the town of Aztec, in New Mexico. This crash supposedly occurred in 1948, but was reported in a book published in 1950 by writer Frank Scully (presumably no relation to FBI agent Dana Scully). This described the recovery of several alien bodies from a crashed silver disc 99 feet across just outside the town of Aztec. The bodies were reported as 'child-like' and about three feet high, which is the other obvious trait of the so-called Greys. When this height and build is added to the facial description from the Hill abduction case, we have a marketing classic that went viral before there was such a thing as viral.

Anyway, over the years, many people have come forward claiming to be witnesses to this recovery, some of whom are even mentioned in the book. This is rather odd, because in 1953 the two conmen who had given the story to Scully in an attempt to sell their 'alien-made' prospecting devices (which claimed to find gas, oil, gold, etc) were convicted of fraud.

It was too late, the story was out there, and could not be recalled. Then again, perhaps the hoax story is itself the hoax, cleverly designed as a double bluff by the shadowy cabal who wishes to keep their dealings with aliens a secret.

There is also another story related to both of these, which suggests that the Roswell crash was caused by a collision between two alien craft in the thunderstorm, and that while one craft disintegrated into fragments, the other crashed more or less intact near the town of Corona (which is actually closer to the ranch in the Roswell case than Roswell is). This craft was supposedly recovered by human military forces, as were the bodies of occupants, who were reported as the familiar Grey aliens.

We Will Destroy Your Planet

At first glance this sounds interesting – a pre-1961 appearance for the Greys, and a more plausible reason – a collision – for a sophisticated interplanetary craft to crash. Physicist Stanton Friedman co-wrote a book on the case, *Crash at Corona*, in 1992, and it has been claimed that material recovered from the ship and reverse-engineered was the source for some current Earth technologies, such as microchips.

Unfortunately, the reports of this incident all date from 1986 or later, and came along with the supposed revelation of the existence of alien-monitoring group Majestic 12, which itself has long since been proved a hoax.

There is, however, a fourth New Mexico case which you may find both interesting and reassuring. On 24 April 1964, near the town of Socorro, a policeman named Lonnie Zamora saw what he thought was a fire near a building used to store dynamite. Investigating, he came upon a landed egg-shaped craft on three legs, which was in the process of being repaired by two child-sized beings in apparent space suits. Some of the brush around them was smouldering. Startled by his appearance, the pair quickly finished up their repairs, boarded their craft, and took off, never to be seen again.

When Zamora investigated the site, he found that sand underfoot had been fused into glass where the craft's exhaust had hit it. Despite further investigations by the police and Air Force, no explanation has ever been confirmed.

At the very least it suggests that repairs in the field are more than possible, if you have the correct equipment and procedures. If the pilots of that craft are reading this, consider yourself congratulated on a job well done.

It may be worth asking why New Mexico in particular is thought to have been an accident black spot for extraterrestrial craft, especially in the late 1940s and early 1950s. The explanations are simple, both from the point of view of motivation for visiting aliens, and for the perceptions of the humans who reported these events.

No Battle Plan Survives First Contact With The Enemy

In 1947, the USAAF base at Roswell was home to the world's only nuclear bomber fleet. The areas around the state, such as White Sands, were for many years used for nuclear testing, and the testing of orbital rockets and ballistic missiles. If you were a human living in that era, the location was surely a troubling one, filled with the promise of future technological change and possible global nuclear holocaust.

If you were an alien observing the Earth at that point, the area was the place with the most potential technological threats to your plans. Either way, it's no real surprise that strange events would be thought of as taking place there.

RENDLESHAM FOREST: Rendlesham Forest is an area of woodland in Surrey, best known in the media today for being the scene of a UFO landing or crash (nobody's quite sure which) report from 1980. In December of that year, several USAF personnel from RAF Woodbridge, on the southern side of the forest, spent several nights investigating an object they believed to have come down nearby.

The incident sparked headlines across the UK, and questions in the British government's House of Commons, but, despite the existence of a tape recording taken by the deputy base commander, all the witnesses tell slightly different stories, so it is impossible to be sure what actually happened. Interestingly, from your military campaign's point of view, the British Ministry of Defence decided that the event was of 'no defence significance', despite the fact that either a) aliens were flying around a base filled with US nuclear warheads and F-111 fighter/bombers, b) unauthorized humans were flying around a base filled with nuclear warheads and planes, or c) the people in charge of looking after nuclear warheads and their warplanes were drunk and/or crazy.

Even the latter option surely ought to have been of extreme significance.

This wasn't the only time Rendlesham had been associated with UFO activity. In 1956, another airbase, RAF Bentwaters, had had to repeatedly scramble interceptors to check out radar tracks of approaching craft.

IN THE EVENT OF CAPTURE

In the event that any of your forces are captured by humans, you will have some time to decide what action to take. You, after all, will have been monitoring Earth's broadcasts into the universe over the past decades, and studying captured specimens. You will therefore have the advantage in being familiar with human communications and psychology.

The humans will have no such head start where communicating with or understanding your species is concerned. (Unless you are also human, from a different era or alternate world. In which case you should continue to employ the same training as you give to any soldier or operative who may become a prisoner.) This means that you can think through your strategy and conduct a measured response, while the human captors are trying to figure out what your personnel actually are.

Do not take too long, however, because it will occur to the humans at some point to vivisect their captive(s), especially if they do not realize that the captives are sentient, or do not recognize their importance to terrestrial science and sociology.

You can simply destroy the holding facility to kill the captives before they can reveal vital facts, or you could mount a rescue mission. Threatening action if they are not released is always a possibility, as is offering a reward or trade. Be aware, though, that making successful communications contact to demand or request the return of any captives will, if this is how you have to announce your existence to humanity, create suspicion, as it will show that you have been monitoring humanity for a long time. Humans will wonder about your motivation in doing so.

As for the captives themselves, of course the first duty of a prisoner is to escape. If you have teleportation technology, all of your forces should be fitted with an internal homing beacon or teleport trigger, which can be used to remove them safely from captivity at any time.

Otherwise, any forces at risk of capture should, as mentioned previously, be trained in escape and evasion techniques and be given a list of rendezvous locations to make for in the event that they can effect an escape by more conventional means.

MAKING YOUR OWN WAY HOME

If no rescue can be mounted, it may be possible for stranded members of your forces – especially those who have survived a crash-landing before your main operation begins – to try making their own way offworld.

If you came through a temporal or dimensional portal, you will need only to travel across the Earth to its location, without being discovered or recaptured. If you came by starship, you will be in a more difficult situation and will have a more difficult travel process ahead of you.

This will entail either constructing a suitable launch facility, which may be well nigh impossible for an individual who isn't a millionaire or making use of one of humanity's launch sites. There are several dozen spaceports on Earth, but most are used only for launching satellites into orbit. Your best choices for making a trip in a suitable vehicle are Kennedy Space Center in Florida and the Baikonur Cosmodrome in Russia. Wenchang Satellite Launch Center in Hainan Province, China, will be a possible option soon, but is not yet operational.

We Will Destroy Your Planet

Needless to say, the few launch sites capable of sending life forms safely into space are well guarded, and there are many restrictions on who gets to take a trip. In general, only qualified military personnel or scientists have been able, after extensive background checks, to be given a seat on even an orbital flight. This is unlikely to be feasible for most extraterrestrials, unless you are able to shapeshift (in which case you can simply choose an astronaut or cosmonaut about to go into space, and imitate them to take their place) or control minds in order to make the relevant authorities give you safe passage.

If you have been stranded and want to try constructing your own suitable launch facility, you will need to be able to either

directly control – through psi power, technology, or chemistry – a lot of humans who can arrange the purchase of land, the construction, security, and so on, or to sell some of your scientific knowledge and technology for a very carefully arranged deal.

You do not need to sell FTL drives, time travel, or doomsday weapons, by the way. Things as simple as new clothing fibres or materials, or heat-resistant or conductive materials will suffice. Such everyday items will both be easier for terrestrial manufacturers to make and market with the minimum of fuss, and be more subtle influences which will not attract attention for being too obviously advanced.

In either event, if you do succeed in making it into orbit by means of a rocket launched from a human spaceport, your problems will really start; humanity has no vessels capable of near-c relativistic travel, let alone FTL or hyperspatial drives. You had best be either very long-lived, because it will take millions of years for you to get anywhere or have suitable suspended animation facilities on board your vehicle.

All you need do then is activate a homing beacon and sleep until one of your ships finds you.

WAR IS MUCH MORE FUN WHEN YOU'RE WINNING

No matter how superior you think you are – or how superior you actually are – there is no such thing as a truly guaranteed victory. It is always possible for you to fail. Remember the story of Musashi and the farmer, and accept that you will lose someday.

The reason why you fail to conquer the Earth could be through bad planning – though hopefully not, now – or sheer bad luck. Perhaps a rival invader or observer of the planet will step in. Perhaps you missed a microbe in your tests, which harmed your forces. Perhaps an unexpected solar flare disabled your ships or equipment. Most likely, if you didn't go with the asteroid bombardment route, you were simply overwhelmingly outnumbered. After all, you can only have as many troops as you can bring or make, while the planetary population has absolutely everyone.

If you have failed in your attempt to conquer the Earth, you will be faced with several options as to what to do next.

EVACUATION

As with all good military planning, it is important to have an exit strategy – or, ideally, more than one, depending on the different circumstances and contexts that might actually require you to withdraw from the Earth. You may wish to evacuate even if you did win the war and conquer the Earth, if you have then gone on to complete all your originally planned operations on the planet and achieved all your objectives. You could have to cease operations on Earth because you've received word of there being more urgent problems at home, or because you are being distracted by a war elsewhere.

More likely, though, if you want to leave, it will be because you have been defeated and sent slinking home with your tails (if you have tails) between your legs (if you have legs). Hopefully this latter case has been avoided if you've been following the advice of this guide correctly.

So, if you can simply leave, do. Make sure that you have not left humanity with any directions to your home, and go find a better target that's less trouble to conquer. You can always re-arm, regroup, reinforce, and come back for a second attempt, but you can be sure that the terrestrial resistance will be waiting for you by the time you return and will have made sure that there are now planetary defences in place.

Depending on how vindictive your nature is, you can carry out a (literal!) scorched Earth policy by either triggering a

No Battle Plan Survives First Contact With The Enemy

nuclear exchange as you go or conducting that by-now very belated asteroid bombardment.

Some means of exit from the planet will be easier than others. If you have come through some kind of fixed portal, be it from another time zone in Earth's past or future, a wormhole link to your home planet, or to a parallel dimension, you obviously have the easiest exit strategy, as you can simply withdraw through the portal on the ground.

Leaving the Earth in a fleet of ships may be a more difficult proposition, especially if your evacuation is due to a defeat by terrestrial military forces. You will need to have suitable assembly and embarkation sites from which your forces can embark on craft designed to carry them out of the gravity well, possibly while still under fire. You may prefer to try negotiating a truce in order to safely embark your forces and leave.

Before you do leave, you should destroy all your technology and equipment that will be left behind, so that humanity cannot use it to follow you for revenge later.

If you can't leave, for whatever reason, or if you just prefer to accept a diplomatic solution – or even if you've been impressed by the humans as worthy opponents – you can sue for peace and negotiate an armistice. This will probably involve you having to make some form of reparations, in the form of reconstruction work and advanced technology.

This is especially possible if the original war for the Earth was sparked by some form of accident or miscommunication, such as human troops shooting your messenger when he emerged from his ship, or you interpreting science fiction TV transmissions as threats that the humans were planning to come and invade you.

It may even be possible that you or some of your forces decide they prefer the terrestrial ways of doing things and decide to stop trying to ruin it, to switch sides, or to outright go native.

Stranger things have happened.

A HISTORY OF ALIEN INVASIONS

According to literature, movies, and TV, the Earth has been under threat of invasion by alien beings for a very long time.

The earliest alien invasion stories are probably religious folk tales from cultures around the world – stories of angels, gods, or other beings coming down from the skies and making lives for themselves on Earth. These usually involve mating with humans, so that idea, of breeding with beings from the skies, has been around for a long time as well.

There are Native American legends of women who came from the stars in flying baskets, but these are largely oral tales, rather than written literature, and, of course, they weren't intended to be tales of invasion. Nor were they intended in any way as science fiction.

We Will Destroy Your Planet

The first (surviving) proper literary fiction example of alien overlords ruling over (literally) parts of the Earth comes in 1727, with Jonathan Swift's famous *Gulliver's Travels*. At one point, Gulliver visits the floating island of Laputa, which is a whole city-state hovering in the air in defiance of gravity, aboard which humanoids who are not human choose to control the weather by blocking sun or rain from reaching the ground below, thus controlling the agriculture of the Earth.

In 1752, Voltaire published *Micromégas*, in which two vast alien intelligences – one from Saturn and one from the star Sirius – visit the earth.

The alien invasion genre isn't really originally a subset of science fiction, however, which was originally developed more with the intent of providing tales of exploration, philosophy and wonder.

It actually evolved from the straightforward genre of invasion literature, which still exists in a far more limited form today, with movies like *Red Dawn*, and, in mutated form, in the zombie apocalypse genre. In general, invasion literature poses as a warning about the dangers of the reader's homeland being overrun by faceless inhuman armies of one kind or another. Invasion literature almost began in the 1790s, after the Montgolfier brothers made their hot air balloon flight (and humans weren't the first passengers of their flying machine, oh no. The first creatures known to have taken successfully to the air over the skies of Earth were nonhumans. On 19 September 1783, the Aérostat *Réveillon* was launched by the Montgolfier brothers, with three passengers: one sheep, one duck, and one rooster. The first manned flight took place a month or so later.)

The French Revolution took place only six years later, and, during the era that followed, of Robespierre's 'Reign of Terror' and the rise of the Emperor Napoleon Bonaparte, there was a brief flurry of stories and even poems in both France and the recently-independent United States of America about using balloons to carry the revolutionary fervour to England.

A History Of Alien Invasions

British writers replied with plays intended to warn about Gallic invasions, such as *The Invasion of England* in 1803, and *The Armed Briton* in 1806. Those were pretty much straightforward propaganda tracts, until the arrival of a proper 'future war' kind of story, in the form of *An Invasion Sketch*, a three-page story which covered a week in Napoleon's supervillain-like conquest of London, in which he rebuilt and renamed the largest British cities. Both sides in the Napoleonic propaganda war then began to make use of the same engravings of fantastical motherships that would soon be used for a French invasion – rafts 2,100 feet on a side, powered by four windmills (one on each corner), with a solid, stone-built castle keep in the middle. To the readers of the early 1800s, this was basically what the sight of giant motherships hovering over cities in *V* or *Independence Day* were to modern TV and movie audiences.

Invasion from above also made its debut here, in the form of engravings, with suitable scaremongering captions and headlines, of fleets of French hot-air balloons floating over the English Channel. The very channel, in fact, whose narrowness made a simple winner-takes-all invasion a focus for centuries.

Almost as soon as the genre had begun, however, the more fanciful invasion-from-the-air and giant-mothership sorts of propaganda were put out of business by Nelson's victory at Trafalgar, which everyone could see pretty much negated the chances of there being any such invasion. (The post-revolutionary French government having executed most of its naval officers on the grounds that anybody and everybody could do the job of an experienced and trained commander equally, didn't do them any favours either.)

At the same time, there was literature that we'd call science fiction, dealing with what the world would be like in the future. *Les Posthumes*, for example, in 1802, *Le Dernier Homme* in 1805, Voss's *Ini: ein Roman aus dem ein und zwanzigsten Jahrhundert* in 1810; and of course Mary

We Will Destroy Your Planet

Shelley's *Frankenstein* in 1818, one of the first true science fiction novels.

As a side note, 1836 brought the first alternate history/ parallel world story covering invasion and conquest: Louis Geoffroy's *Napoléon et la conquête du monde (1812—1832): Histoire de la Monarchie universelle*. This tells of Bonaparte being victorious in Russia, conquering Britain, Asia and the Americas, until the whole world accepts him as their Universal Monarch.

Such tales were not particularly popular or memorable, and the potential genre sank without much of a trace, while Gothic literature swept across the pages of English-language printers and bookshelves, and held sway for decades. Eighty years later, however, things changed.

In 1870, Prussia (part of Germany) took on France, who in the Napoleonic era had itself occupied the various German kingdoms in a hostile fashion. The Prussians armed themselves with far more modern technology than the French forces had. The Prussians had equipped themselves with a more modern army, lower-visibility uniforms, rifled barrels in all their weapons, breech-loading artillery that was much faster to reload, armoured ships and carriages, troop trains, and telegraphs for communication. The Prussians made swift victories with their superior training and technology, and Britain, in particular, took note that the face of warfare had just changed. Papers, magazines and books all raced to say their piece about the new warfare, but the one that grabbed popular public attention was a fictional story, a pamphlet called *The Battle of Dorking*.

Written for political reasons by George Chesney, the story tells in flashback of a successful invasion of England at Dorking by an unnamed (but obviously German) foreign power. The viewpoint character is constantly pursued by technologically superior invaders, while his own side are badly equipped and untrained by comparison. Chesney, though an experienced military officer himself, had actually borrowed much of his writing style and plot structure from two historical novels about the Napoleonic wars, *The Conscript* (1864) and its sequel, *Waterloo* (1865), by Erckmann-Chatrian, and it's a format and tone that would work very well – and very recognizably – for H. G. Wells some 28 years later.

The Battle of Dorking was a huge hit, and was immediately followed not just by a genre of invasion-by-technological-and-military-superiority but various unofficial sequels and ripostes, copyright be damned.

Also in 1871, Edward Bulwer-Lytton published another now legendary invasion story, *The Coming Race*, which dealt with the first sort-of alien invasion. In this story, the alien invaders, the Deros, are not from outer space, but from a subterranean realm under the Earth's own surface. Strangely, though largely forgotten as an early science fiction novel, the story sparked a rather odd conspiracy theory that flourished between the 1890s and the 1960s, in which many people believed that the Deros, or at least some sort of underground race, actually existed, and that the Earth was hollow.

Most of these tales were, however, simply about other nations invading, and the atrocities they could be expected to commit. In 1898, H. G. Wells changed all that forever and invented a whole new genre.

Wells took the tone of *The Battle of Dorking*, the Gothic futurism of some of those other European novels, and a subversive attitude towards colonialism (brave at the time, when the British Empire was the largest empire the Earth has ever seen), and blended them with science, to produce the now legendary *War of the Worlds*.

In Wells's book, aliens from the planet Mars invade the Earth, treating the natives like cattle and trying to rebuild the planet in the image of their own – decades before words like terraforming had been coined. Wells had in mind to refer to the way the colonial powers of the 19th century had treated

We Will Destroy Your Planet

India and Africa, but what he ended up doing was pretty much inventing one of the 20th and (so far) 21st centuries' most popular forms of entertainment. Interestingly, Wells didn't realise this himself at the time. He didn't consider himself a science fiction writer, not least because the phrase 'science fiction' itself wasn't coined for another 20 years or so. In fact, Wells later wrote several other more straightforward invasion stories, which veered towards the futurist, warning of military technology and applications to come.

Actually, the first true alien invasion story as we know the term is not the more famous *War of the Worlds*, but *The Germ Growers*, by Robert Potter, which was published in Australia in 1892. Potter has his aliens masquerade as human and set up a biowarfare programme, intending to develop a virus which will wipe out humanity, leaving the planet free to be taken over by their species. Which, to be fair, is the plot of a fair number of *Doctor Who* episodes, especially those written by Terry Nation.

The next stage of the alien invasion genre came from the US. This is perhaps unsurprising, as the popularity of Wells's novel had led a number of American newspaper publishers to commission their own sequels to *War of the Worlds*, which brought the invasion to America, and took the fight back to Mars. In the first years of the 20th century, rip-offs abounded, though these became less popular during the years of the First World War.

In the 1920s and '30s, however, science fiction, inspired by so much post-war technological development, boomed. With it, so did the alien invasion. The futurism of science exploration blended with the vicarious thrills of the pulp era to produce franchises such as Tarzan (who also fought creatures from a hollow Earth), Flash Gordon, and Buck Rogers. Killer Kane and Ming the Merciless embarked on their campaigns to crush the forces of Earth. In print, strange aliens from far corners of the galaxy set their sights on Earth in the works of E. E. 'Doc' Smith and others.

A History Of Alien Invasions

To be fair, most of these villains were, like the invaders of the earlier European invasion literature, thinly disguised racist stereotypes, usually of the Asiatic variety. This isn't surprising, as invasion stories have always been about fear of the incomer who isn't part of the local group.

War of the Worlds again changed that, this time in the form of a radio drama produced by Orson Welles. This 1938 Halloween broadcast is the alien invasion story to which all others still aspire, having caused a number of listeners to believe that three-legged Martian war machines really were trashing New Jersey.

Rather than disappearing during the Second World War, as invasion literature had done during the First World War, the alien invasion story simply took more overt sides, with alien invaders in the pulps and comics siding with the Axis forces in stories, which merely served to give the heroes all the more reason to fight against the villains.

Thanks to both Wells and the pulps and comics, the alien invasion had become a staple of written SF by the 1930s. The sub-genre would become more accessible to a wider audience, however, on screen.

It didn't take long for Flash Gordon and Buck Rogers to become Saturday morning serial films, bringing their alien invaders to cinemas everywhere, but what sparked the next shift in the genre was the Cold War and the rise of the UFO report. The year 1947 was a good one for UFOs, with the first reported sighting of so-called (by a reporter, not by the witness) flying saucers, and the original Roswell incident. Over the next few years, flying saucers from space were big news, hitting front pages in the US on a regular basis, and making massed flypasts over Washington DC in 1952. Couple that with the Cold War paranoia about Communism, and the fear of the devastation caused by the all-new nuclear technology, and what do you get?

We Will Destroy Your Planet

You got a golden age of alien invasion movies, in which Communists of some form or another (either politically, just being from the Red planet or being generally faceless) came to the USA and caused havoc. *Earth vs. the Flying Saucers, Invaders from Mars,* the George Pal movie version of *War of the Worlds*, *The Thing from Another World*, and many more such movies graced the screens.

The genre also mutated somewhat, with the related alien infiltration genre coming to prominence in both literature and film. The likes of Jack Finney's 1954 novel *The Bodysnatchers*, filmed several times and better known as *Invasion of the Bodysnatchers*, and Robert Heinlein's *The Puppet Masters* (1951) ushered in the popular theme of alien conquest by infiltration rather than overt warfare. Because these books and movies came to prominence at the time of the Cold War, during the height of the McCarthy Hearings and the paranoia that anyone could secretly be a Communist spy for the Soviets, this whole side of the genre has become viewed as an allegory for that fear.

It's certainly true in some cases – *The Puppet Masters* repeatedly compares the invading parasites directly to Russia and Communism – but this is an interpretation attributed more by critics and audiences than by the creators. For example, the 1956 film version of *Invasion of the Bodysnatchers* is often held to be the definitive Reds-under-the-beds paranoia allegory, but writer Jack Finney, producer Walter Mirisch, director Don Siegel, and star Kevin McCarthy all maintained that no such thing was intended.

In the UK, alien invaders were almost as popular, but less open to interpretation as being based on fear of Communism as they were clearly highlighting the wounds of the recent war and the loss of Empire. Where America feared the soulless commune from outer space, Britain was wary of the dangers of German-inspired rocket technology in the Quatermass serials, and of the resurgence of Nazism in the form of the Daleks.

A History Of Alien Invasions

The other big difference between alien invasions on American and British screens is that American media tended to put alien invasion stories on the cinema screen – or at least at the drive-in theatre – while British invaders were far more likely to threaten the heroes of TV shows than films. Partly this may be because American SF series tended to be more about the pioneer spirit, going out and exploring, while their movies were more about bringing thrills to an audience. It also probably relates to the fact that British cinema simply never was as big on SF movies, while TV, needing more hours of programming to fill, could be more imaginative.

Oddly, while the 'other' or alien that Hollywood feared in the 1950s was supposedly in the form of Communism, the Eastern Bloc made its own SF movies, which were far less driven by fear. This means they tended not to be invasion stories in the typical sense, but were usually about human explorers going to other planets (Venus was a common destination) and there meeting utopian alien civilizations who either already were communist themselves or were happy to learn about it.

This probably has less to do with the values of the political system itself, or even the state-mandated propaganda side of things, and more to do with the effects of having gone through a lot of very bloody recent history, up to and including the Nazi invasion of the Second World War.

In fact, it's worth noting that the country that really took the alien invasion genre to heart and made it a major part of the entertainment media was the one big player in the Second World War that was never threatened with invasion, let alone actually invaded.

Britain had been under threat of invasion for the first three years or so of the war, and its alien invasion stories tended to either reflect the recent fascist threat, or be more subtle types of invasion of the land of the living that had evolved from ghost stories and demonology. Japan had been occupied by the US, and its fictional alien invaders tended to be technologically superior powers who stayed remote and used monsters of mass destruction that reflected both the nuclear bomb and the constant threat of earthquakes and tsunami.

Throughout all these different periods and fashions of storytelling, H. G. Wells's *War of the Worlds* has still remained the touchstone for the alien invasion story. It has been reinvented for every generation. A Hollywood movie with Oscar-winning visual effects in the 1950s, which relocated the story to contemporary America (as had Orson Welles's radio version), was followed by a jingoistic sequel TV series in the late 1980s. A Steven Spielberg remake a few years ago tried to make it more a tale of obstacles keeping a shattered family apart. Whether it is Jeff Wayne's unofficial, haunting musical version, or a big screen adaptation, *War of the Worlds* still casts its long shadow. *Mars Attacks*, which started as a trading card series in the 1950s, before becoming a comic book series and movie in the 90s, and still going strong in card and comic format today, is a black-humoured pastiche. The Martians may come in flying saucers rather than cylinders, but they have their heat-rays all present and correct. The blockbuster *Independence Day* even managed to update the virus idea, by using a computer virus uploaded from a laptop to knock out the systems in the alien mothership, leading to the defeat of their invasion.

V and *Independence Day* share an ethos that dramatic imagery is preferable to practicality or sense. Both invasions begin with gigantic saucers hovering over the cities of the Earth, making for jaw-dropping visuals that certainly impress both the characters and the audience, but which would be rather foolish for an actual invader, who would surely rather keep their plans and presence a secret until they actually attack.

Alien invasions have not always been depicted as necessarily hostile or evil, however, and there is a whole sub-

A History Of Alien Invasions

genre of the benevolent invasion, exemplified by Arthur C. Clarke's *Childhood's End*, in which the aliens are seeking to better humanity. Both versions of the film *The Day the Earth Stood Still* threaten this, as the aliens there are concerned about humanity and human effects on the galaxy at large.

Oddly, SF has more recently taken a turn back towards the more paranoid style of alien invasions, but this time with religiously radicalized terrorists with suicide bombs in mind as the threat to be converted into hostile aliens for the purposes of entertainment.

The alien invasion genre has also adapted over time to new forms of media. From books it moved to films. When radio and TV came along, aliens invaded the new formats very quickly. Nowadays the alien invasion genre is hugely popular in video games, second only to military shooters and racing games, at least in the West.

This is perhaps not surprising, as the game that really sparked the video game medium itself was an alien invasion game - the legendary *Space Invaders*.

The other unusual form of alien invasion story that is seen to subvert the usual genre is the fake invasion. This is a story in which an apparent alien invasion is actually intended to unite humanity against a (non-existent) common enemy. The most famous example is probably the giant squid at the end of Alan Moore's graphic novel *Watchmen*, though this element is left out of the movie version.

Moore has been criticized for supposedly taking the idea from the *Architects of Fear* episode of *The Outer Limits*, but in fact this type of faux invasion has a longer history than that. Theodore Sturgeon originated the idea in the short story *Unite and Conquer* in 1948, while Kurt Vonnegut used it as the basis for his full-length novel *The Sirens of Titan* in 1959.

There have actually been several suggestions in real life that this strategy should be tried. In 1983, US President Ronald Reagan suggested in a broadcast that the US and the then Soviet Union would unite against an alien invasion. In 2011, Paul Krugman suggested that building defences against potential alien invasion could spur financial growth in the world's economies. The alien invasion *story* may not just be fiction for long, even if the aliens themselves are.

THE BEST OF THE INVASIONS

The best fictional invasions will be valuable research and inspiration for both invaders and defenders, so here is a quick rundown of those that are worth experiencing.

CONQUERING THE EARTH IN PRINT

Some memorable or important alien invasion novels, which should be read by anyone with an interest in either attacking or defending the Earth:

WAR OF THE WORLDS (H. G. Wells): The definitive alien invasion novel from which all others take their lead. Originally published in 1898, the nameless narrator's tale of travelling through an English countryside besieged by Martians still holds up today. The novel is short, but introduces so many of both the familiar elements and ones well thought-out according to the science of the time: the arrival of a technologically and militarily superior adversary, battles in which the cream of Earth's military are outclassed, the bravery and tragedy of the collateral damage, aliens using humans for food, terraforming by means of Martian plant life (the Red Weed) altering the atmosphere... it's all here.

THE PUPPET MASTERS (Robert Heinlein): A quite exciting

little adventure, in which a secret agent discovers that some of the enemy spies and saboteurs he has been hunting are from rather further away than Russia. In fact they are parasitic aliens that control people. This is the granddaddy of all alien parasite stories, of course, and the likes of the writers who created the Goa'uld in *Stargate* owe it quite a debt.

THE BODY SNATCHERS (Jack Finney): Almost as definitive as Wells's expose of colonialist military invasion, but covering a stealthier attempt to conquer the Earth. As with Wells's book, the story is told by a first person narrator, but this story is more unsettling, perhaps. If you're only familiar with the film versions – official and unofficial – you'll find that the original book has a clearer picture of the ultimate threat to life on Earth, as the invaders cannot reproduce, but only have a five-year lifespan, meaning the Earth would be sterile after that.

CHILDHOOD'S END (Arthur C. Clarke): This is an example of the benevolent rule of a successful invader, in which the story is told by a person who serves the Overlords, demonic-looking beings who actually invaded the Earth in order to prevent humanity from turning to the Dark Side and conquering the universe. This they achieve by enlightening humanity, at least to start with… As with all of Clarke's work, it is thought out with scientific precision, and contains some interesting reversals and characterization of the effects of an invasion on both human society and the invaders.

FOOTFALL (Larry Niven and Jerry Pournelle): This reinvents the alien invasion for the 1980s, with a doorstop-sized epic in which pachydermic aliens use sensible strategies like research and asteroid bombardment in an attempt to conquer the Earth. Not all of their attempts at research are successful, as proven when they think they can learn about humanity well enough from notorious 1970s blue movie, *Deep Throat*.

We Will Destroy Your Planet

As well as having epic action, and terrifyingly believable asteroid strikes, *Footfall* does a good job of depicting the invaders as having an alien mindset, and inability to understand humanity – who to them, are the incomprehensible aliens.

WORLDWAR (Harry Turtledove): This is a series of military SF pseudo-historicals in which reptilian aliens invade the Earth at the same time as the Second World War breaks out. The series delves into the relative political and moral developments that would have occurred in such a situation, as well as being action-packed.

THE DAY OF THE TRIFFIDS (John Wyndham) is worth mentioning, as it does cover the events that occur when an alien species – the Triffids, a race of mobile carnivorous plants – begins to spread and multiply on Earth. This species is not extraterrestrial in nature, however (the narrator explicitly states this), but almost certainly an artificial creation from a Soviet lab.

WE CONTROL YOUR TV SET

Aliens have been invading our TV sets for years – and these stories have been broadcast into the universe at large, so who knows who may be watching these memorable examples?

QUATERMASS II (October–November 1955): This six-part BBC serial dealt with the discovery of an invasion of parasites that had already been in progress for some years. Like *The Puppet Masters* it deals with parasitic aliens – with a collective consciousness – who control human minds into building environmental facilities for them. They plan to terraform the Earth later, until the scientists working on a new rocket uncover their plan. This series, like many British alien invasion stories, echoes the Nazi threat from the Second World War, with work camps, black-uniformed guards, and bomb-like objects falling from the skies on peaceful English towns (these objects actually bring the alien parasites).

The story was remade by Hammer films in 1957, but this changes the ending, so that, rather than terraforming the Earth, the aliens have been growing giant blob-like life forms which burst free into the countryside. The serial also inspired (to put it politely) many invasions in the later series *Doctor Who*, in some cases literally shot-for-shot.

Note that there is also an invasion of sorts in the following Quatermass serial, *Quatermass and the Pit*, though this invasion is actually a delayed effect from the original landing five million years earlier, and the 'invaders' are just the segment of the human population who have the genetic memories of the long-dead aliens (who are, yes, Martians again).

THE MONSTERS ARE DUE ON MAPLE STREET (*The Twilight Zone*, March 1960): This episode of the legendary anthology series depicts not an outright military alien invasion, but some intelligent preparatory strategy on the part of the aliens, and good observation of human group reactions and psychology. In the episode, the aliens simply let their ship be glimpsed briefly, cut the power to a residential area, and let the residents react as they feel appropriate – which means suspicion, tribalism, and eventually violence. As an example of the divide-and-conquer strategy, it is worth giving thought to.

TO SERVE MAN (*The Twilight Zone*, 1962): Based on a short story by Damon Knight from 1950, this is a good example of the apparently benevolent alien arrival, which conceals a secret objective to turn humanity into food resources. Much of its original power depends on the twist over the double meaning of the word 'serve' in the alien documentation, and this twist became sufficiently widespread in pop culture that it would no longer be a surprise today, but it still shows a well thought-out plan of deceptive conquest.

THE ARCHITECTS OF FEAR (*The Outer Limits*, 1963): This technically isn't an alien invasion, but an example of the fake one created by scientists hoping to scare humanity into making peace during the Cold War.

THE DALEK INVASION OF EARTH (*Doctor Who*, 1964): This is only the second serial to feature the Daleks, and the first of their many attempts to invade the Earth in the past, present, or future. In this story, the Daleks attempt to replace the magnetic core of the Earth with a power unit, which is not a very practical idea. The idea of Daleks invading the Earth, and the sights of them having famous London landmarks all to themselves – the first time very nonhuman aliens had been shown so convincingly in real locations on screen – was so popular with viewers, however, that not only did they try to invade in several other stories, but this story was remade as a cinema film, which tells the same story, with more fun, in about a third of the time.

Though the story begins well into the Daleks' occupation of the planet after a successful invasion, dialogue establishes that they did use sensible strategies for their attack, however crazy their ultimate objective is. We hear that they began with a meteor bombardment to destroy defensive infrastructures, followed by biological warfare to reduce the native population to manageable levels for enslavement.

See also the stories, *The Daleks' Masterplan* (1966), *Evil of the Daleks* (1967), *Day of the Daleks* (1972), *Resurrection of the Daleks* (1984), *Remembrance of the Daleks* (1988), *The Parting of the Ways* (2005), *Doomsday* (2006), *Evolution of the Daleks* (2007), and *The Stolen Earth* (2008). In these later stories, the Daleks have been seen to (among other things) set up a client state to use slaves to strip the Earth of resources, bomb the

A History Of Alien Invasions

Earth with nuclear weapons and asteroids, develop mind control, adapt themselves to flying over obstacles, and conduct a mass military invasion on-screen.

THE INVASION (*Doctor Who*, 1968): The second most popular and familiar hostile aliens in *Doctor Who* are the Cybermen, a race of cyborgs in need of fresh converts. In their own minds, the Cybermen think of themselves as benevolent, removing fear and hatred from humans when they convert them into mostly-robots. (If this sounds awfully like the Borg in *Star Trek*, you'd be right.) In their first story, *The Tenth Planet*, the Cybermen pilot their home planet (which has a power unit – why didn't the Daleks just steal that one?) to Earth in order to drain it of energy, and invade the Earth with a mere 250 spaceships containing half a dozen Cybermen each – far too small a force to achieve the success depicted. In this later story, however, they display far superior strategic thinking, by allying themselves with a multinational corporation which can use their technology to render humanity unconscious, and thus allow the Cybermen to invade unopposed from their position in the lunar L2 position.

In a later story, *Army of Ghosts* (2006), five million Cybermen use a dimensional portal to transition through from a parallel world, displaying the value of using such a home position from which to launch an invasion. This episode also demonstrates the risks of random outside factors causing the invasion to fail, and how an invader may need to ally with their intended victims when a rival and superior invader tries to join in the fun.

THE INVADERS (1967–68): The last real gasp of the Reds-under-the-beds style of 1950s SF, this series was about an architect who discovered that humanoid aliens were secretly infiltrating the Earth in order to take it over. It's really more a remix of *The Fugitive* than anything else, but the photography, mood, and some of the quirks of the aliens and their distinctive flying saucers are especially memorable still.

The series was an obvious influence on the story arcs running through the later *The X-Files*, and a miniseries remake was made in 1995.

U.F.O. (1970): This 26-episode British series takes a surprisingly gritty approach and plotline, prefiguring some elements of *The X-Files* as much as *The Invaders* does. In this series, Earth is under constant threat and visits from aliens who abduct humans to harvest their organs, in order to allow their pilots to survive. The aliens are limited in number, with only two to a ship, and so must operate by stealth. Believably, the aliens must wear environment suits at all times, and even have their suits filled with breathable oxygenated liquid to cushion against G-forces and variant pressures in the atmosphere and at sea. (It is also implied at least once that the 'aliens' seen are in fact converted enslaved humans, and that the genuine aliens may be parasitic or even non-corporeal.) Humanity's defences are a secret organization called SHADO, which is based in a movie studio.

V (1984): This event miniseries intended to lure audiences away from the Los Angeles Olympics changed the direction of all on-screen alien invasions. Gone were the days of stealthy UFOs being seen by characters who would never be believed, or aliens infiltrating by stealth. In *V*, spectacle was the order of the day, as the Visitors parked their motherships above major cities, and began to announce that they had come to help. In reality, of course, they were lizards intending to steal the Earth's water, and use humans for food.

The series covered various themes – the Holocaust, fascism, use of humans as cattle, action-adventure, interspecies attraction, factions within the aliens who preferred Earth's ways, you name it. It picked and chose from the themes and tropes seen in alien invasion stories up to that date, and essentially produced a 'best of' compilation. It was one of the most successful miniseries ever, and paved the way for a sequel miniseries, *V: The Final Battle*, a *V: The Series* of 19 episodes, and a two-season remake in 2010–11.

THE X-FILES (1993–2002): This series about FBI agents wasn't solely an invasion story, as it covered various other types of paranormal, science fiction, and horror genre storylines, but it is perhaps best remembered for its ongoing story arcs regarding aliens planning to invade the Earth and colonize it.

There seemed to be several different types of aliens in the show, with different plans for invasion: there were Greys abducting people, a life form in the form of a viscous black oil which possessed people, cloned aliens who intended to colonize the planet with other clones, aliens who may have engineered humanity to be their invaders by proxy, and so on. The end result was a series that often featured stories involving the various different tropes of alien invasion, but in a self-contradictory way that didn't quite hold together.

Nevertheless, many episodes are valuable and entertaining depictions of stealthy invasion plans and historical UFO reports.

BUSTING THE BLOCK

Even outside the home, wandering the streets of Earth's cities, there is no escape from invading aliens, who are regular gatecrashers in the world's cinemas. Ten movie invasions worthy of note include the following:

EARTH VS THE FLYING SAUCERS (1956): A scientist working on a satellite launching programme is concerned by both the number of his satellites which are disappearing, and by being buzzed in his car by a UFO. It turns out that the

We Will Destroy Your Planet

UFOs are responsible for destroying the satellites, which they thought were attacks upon them. After two aliens are killed by gunfire, a fleet of flying saucers attack the Earth and begin destroying major landmarks…

This movie is important in many ways. The effects were done by the late Ray Harryhausen, better known for mythologically-based stop-motion monsters, while the invaders' tactics and science are well thought-out and prescient. Their ships, for example, use magnetic fields to fly, and relativistic time dilation at near-c speeds is used. They use the ability to induce solar flares as weapons to disable terrestrial communications, they have what we would now call Wikipedia.

Contemporary UFO lore is also present and correct, as is the influence of Wells's book, in the form of heat rays that disintegrate enemies and vehicles. Overall, this is a seminal alien invasion work.

INVADERS FROM MARS (1953): This is a surrealist effort that prefigures a lot of later alien invasions on screen. It features a lead character who sees the aliens but isn't believed, humans abducted and put under alien control (well before this began to be claimed by people in real life), and so on. As with *War of the Worlds*, the aliens are Martians, and have battles with military (in extensive and excessive stock footage).

The movie is visually striking and memorable, for all its lack of budget, even with its appalling 'it was all a dream' ending. It does succeed in building a disturbing mood and some effective tension, while the aliens display good sense for a unit of limited force by concealing themselves and making use of controlled human proxies. Once seen, it is not forgotten.

A remake was produced in 1986, but this was largely played for laughs, and didn't have the sense to leave out the silly ending.

A History Of Alien Invasions

WAR OF THE WORLDS (1953): The first film version of Wells's novel is easily the best, though Jeff Wayne's musical version is the best adaptation overall. In the movie, the main character is not a journalist and observer, but a scientist seeking to defeat the invaders. Although the plotline is a loose adaptation, and many elements changed from the novel, this film does manage to convey the *mood* and feel of the novel, by cherry-picking elements and vignettes to keep, and building a straightforward defend-against-alien-invaders story around them.

As in the novel, the Martians crash-land their vessels on Earth, fight the (contemporary US) army, harvest humans, and are defeated by microbial life. There is no mention of the Red Weed, however, and the film lacks the anti-colonialist and secularist subtexts.

There have been several remakes, ranging from low-budget amateur adaptations of the novel, to Spielberg's horribly misjudged 2005 version, which manages not to actually show the battles of the war. (The clue's in the name, guys.)

The 1990s also saw a TV sequel series, which ran for two seasons.

INVASION OF THE BODYSNATCHERS (1956): Don Siegel's film version of Jack Finney's novel is a slow-boiling film noir kind of alien invasion, with a steadily increasing atmosphere of strangeness and paranoia, and is well worth viewing. The pod people aliens themselves are perhaps best thought of as a form of biological weapon or a force of nature – because rather than colonizing the Earth for themselves, they would all die off and leave the planet ripe for re-occupation – and it's interesting to speculate on whether there was another species of alien masterminds behind it all.

The story and its atmosphere have been so definitive that there have been many remakes, both officially and unofficially. Officially acknowledged remakes are the grittier 1978 version under the same title, *Body Snatchers* (1993), and *The Invasion*

We Will Destroy Your Planet

(2007). Unofficial, or at least unacknowledged, remakes include *The Faculty* (1998).

DESTROY ALL MONSTERS (1968): This is actually intended as a special anniversary movie for Toho's kaiju series, as it was the 20th movie in the series, which is why it includes so many of the monsters: Godzilla, Rodan, Mothra, King Ghidorah, and seven others. It is, however, still an alien invasion movie.

In this film, the invading Kilaak race take control of the Earth's giant monsters, and use them to attack cities around the world. It makes sense that the Kilaaks would need to use local power to conduct their attack, as they only have one ship conducting their campaign.

As alien invasion movies go, this one has more big-budget destruction than any other, until perhaps *Independence Day*, as Tokyo, Beijing, Moscow, New York, Paris and London all get stomped on and torn apart.

SUPERMAN II (1980): Although this isn't obviously recognizable as an alien invasion movie, it absolutely is one, and takes a slightly different approach than usual by depicting a successful conquest of the Earth by a tiny group who have huge innate powers rather than strategy or military strength– the three Kryptonian individuals, General Zod, Non, and Ursa.

In reality, however, it should be noted that their invasion is not planned in advance, and is basically an opportunist raid for personal gratification, with no real objective clearly visible. In this respect, it actually shares a certain mood with the invaders of *Mars Attacks!*

INDEPENDENCE DAY (1996): Like the TV miniseries *V* before it, this large-scale SF disaster movie basically takes many tropes and elements from prior alien invasion books, TV shows, and movies. This straightforward invasion action/

disaster movie takes the motherships-over-cities from *V*, the vulnerability to a type of virus from the perception of *War of the Worlds*, the destruction of major landmarks from *Earth vs. the Flying Saucers*, and so on and so forth, and makes an entertaining spectacle out of it all.

Oddly, though, rather than launching a fashion for a revived sub-genre of alien invasion movies, this actually sparked a fashion for disaster movies in which major – especially US – cities are destroyed in glorious and realistic detail.

It is still, however, the perfect go-to movie for alien invasion fun.

MARS ATTACKS! (1996): Based on the trading card series, this movie depicts an alien military attack with sheer joy of destruction for recreational purposes as the objective, rather than taking over a world for resources or living space.

DISTRICT 9 (2009): Not strictly an invasion movie – as the aliens are stranded refugees rather than invaders – but still a very believable story of what happens when there is a sizeable alien population on Earth, and the tensions that result. In many ways it is comparable to the movie and TV series *Alien Nation*, but that franchise is more simply a buddy–cop story with an alien.

BATTLE: LOS ANGELES (2011): In a change to the usual type of film in which scientists and heroes work out a way to send the alien invaders packing, this is a grittier effort showing the life of the ordinary front-line soldier in a battle to defend the Earth from invasion. As more of a vignette rather than the complete story of an invasion from attack to final repulsion of the enemy, this is a nice change of view.

YOU WIN OR YOU DIE

Ordinary humans of all ages can, of course, practice their skills at repelling alien invaders at any time.

SPACE INVADERS (1978): The original alien invasion video game basically invented video gaming. It was a simple yet addictive set-up, which is still popular on many consoles and smartphones today. In essence, the player controls a little tank at the bottom of the screen, sheltering under houses in order to shoot at waves of descending alien invaders who are dropping bombs. The aliens get faster as they descend.

The game was surprisingly addictive, perhaps due to the instinctive game play, but perhaps also due to the simple but very distinctive music/sound effect.

A History Of Alien Invasions

X-COM: ENEMY UNKNOWN (1994): This is a strategy game about defending the Earth from aliens who are abducting humans, and has both a larger map-based strategy mode, and a closer squad-based tactical simulation mode.

The game spawned several sequels, with varying types of game play, from arcade flight simulation to first-person shooter, and is currently being relaunched for today's consoles. The original is still the best, though.

DUKE NUKEM 3D (1995): A rude, crude, and surprisingly funny foul-mouthed first-person shooter in which the player character roams around various city and desert settings, eventually going to space, in his quest to save the world from aliens who have invaded in order to steal women.

Despite being famous for its immature humour, there are many interesting elements to its alien invasion theme: different types of aliens use sensible equipment like jetpacks and invisibility cloaks. There are different aliens adapted to different environments, and also there are visual, auditory, and plot references to many different SF franchises, including the *Alien* series.

HALF-LIFE (1998): The Half-Life series has the player-character, a physicist named Gordon Freeman, fighting against aliens who invaded through a dimensional portal that had been accidentally created between Earth and their world during an experiment at a secret military research facility. Several different alien races invaded through the portal, and in the sequel, *Half-Life 2*, others turn out to have come in ships in the interim.

This series covers many bases, from dimensional transference, insectoid aliens, one set of invaders joining forces with humanity, giant tripod walking machines, resource-stripping of the planet, parasitic aliens, enslavement of zombified humans... It has pretty much everything.

We Will Destroy Your Planet

DESTROY ALL HUMANS (2005): Yes, you get to be a Grey alien who can roam around abducting humans, throwing cows around the place, and blowing up stuff on Earth. All of which is tremendous fun.

RESISTANCE: FALL OF MAN (2006): Like the *Worldwar* book series, this game presents an alternate history in which an infectious telepathic gestalt alien begins to invade Earth during the Second World War. It is unclear whether the Chimaera are extraterrestrials, extradimensional, or created by human experimentation, but they are clearly an alien invader.